Shays' Rebellion

At dusk Peter came in from the cowshed. He was still angry at Sheriff Porter and Major Mattoon, but he'd worked some of his anger off. "That's one thing about getting into a temper," he said. "It gets a lot of wood cut."

We sat down to supper—milk, johnnycake, cheese, and boiled eggs. Molly waited until Peter had stoked up at little bit. "What are you going to do about the oxen?" she said.

"Shoot somebody," he said.

"Peter," Molly said sharply. "I don't want any of that talk, even in jest."

"I'm not joking," he said. "I fought one war, I can fight another."

"Stop it," she said. "You'll scare the little ones."

He looked at the children. "You're not scared, are you?"

They shook their heads. I could see that they were scared, though. "Peter," I said, "I don't see how we can run the farm without the oxen."

"I know," he said. "We're going to get them back."

"How?"

"We're going over to see Daniel Shays," he said. "Maybe he and I'll shoot somebody together."

**Also by James Lincoln Collier
and Christopher Collier,
available from Point:**

My Brother Sam Is Dead
The Bloody Country

THE WINTER HERO

James Lincoln Collier & Christopher Collier

SCHOLASTIC INC.

New York Toronto London Auckland Sydney

ISBN 0-590-41533-6

12 11 10 9 8 7 6 5 4 3 2 1   7 8 9/8 0 1 2/9

Printed in the U.S.A.   01

For our Massachusetts connection,
Lydia, Willie, Paul, and Susan

Chapter One

I RAN ACROSS THE BACK FIELD AS FAST AS I could go, heading for the woodlot where Peter was cutting firewood. It was late in the afternoon, but it was hot, the way it can be in August in New England. As I got up toward the tree line I could smell the grapes on the vines climbing up through the branches. I couldn't see Peter, but I could hear the saw going buzz, buzz on each stroke. "Peter," I shouted.

The saw stopped for a few seconds and then it started up again. I was nearly at the woodlot now. "Peter," I shouted. The saw stopped again. I got to the fence at the end of the field and climbed over it into the woods. Now I could see Peter through the trees, standing there with the bucksaw in his hands, three-foot logs scattered on the ground around him. He stood watching as I ran through the trees. "Peter, he's taking the oxen."

"What? What's happening?"

I came up to him and stood in front of him, panting. He was more than six feet tall and I wasn't but five-foot-five. "The oxen. He's taking them."

"Who's—"

"The sheriff. Sheriff Porter."

His head snapped back as if he had been hit, and then his jaw jutted forward the way it did when he started to lose his temper. "Let's go," he said. He flung the saw off onto the woodpile and started running. I picked up the saw. It would rust if it was left out overnight. You could spend half a day sharpening the teeth if that happened. I couldn't even guess how many shillings a new blade would cost. I put the saw over my shoulder with the teeth facing away from my neck so I wouldn't get cut if I tripped. Then I began to run. Peter was far ahead of me. He was strong and he was a fast runner, and by the time I got clear of the shade of the woodlot he was nearly across the back field. I ran on. I saw him vault the fence into the barnyard and disappear around the side of the barn. By the time I got to the fence myself I could hear him shouting at somebody. I climbed over the fence carefully so as not to get nicked by the saw, went around the barn, and leaned the saw against the barn door.

The barn was about fifty feet behind the house. In between there was the hen house, the hog pen, and a patch of ground where Molly grew her squash and beans and pumpkins and such. The sheriff was standing in front of the barn next to his horse. He had got the oxen out of the barn, yoked them together, and was running lines from the yoke to the horse's harness. It was going to take him hours to lead the oxen anyplace that way.

Peter stood there, standing as tall as he could to loom over the sheriff. "Take your hands off them," he said.

"Peter, don't give me trouble," Sheriff Porter said. "Do you think I like this?" There was a musket hanging down next to the horse's saddle, and he gave it a quick look.

Peter reached out, grabbed the sheriff's forearm, and squeezed it. "Mattoon sent you."

The sheriff looked back at Peter, pretty calm. "Never mind Mattoon," he said. "I have a legal order to take these oxen."

"Signed by Mattoon."

"He's a justice of the peace. It's legal."

"It may be legal, but it's not right. How am I going to plow without oxen?"

Molly was standing at the back door, watching. She was holding the baby in her arms and the other two little ones were peeking out from behind her. "Peter," she hollered. "Hold your temper."

Peter gave her a look, and then turned back to the sheriff. "I'm warning you, Porter," he said. "Cut these oxen loose or I'll break you in half."

He could do it, too; he was that strong. The sheriff stopped tying the rope and stared at Peter. "Look," he said, "I don't like this either. It's the law. You borrowed money from Mattoon and you didn't pay him. He's got a legal right to take the oxen."

"As the law he signs the order; as my creditor he takes my oxen," Peter shouted. "How can I pay anybody anything when every time I turn around Mattoon and his kind in the General Court have plastered on another tax?"

"Peter, hold your temper," Molly said.

"You're not the only one," Sheriff Porter said. "Yesterday I took a horse and a plow from James Bacon and the day before, a hundred weight of flax from Hezakiah White. And last week we had to foreclose on a farm down in Amherst. I didn't like any of it, either, Peter, but that's the law."

"Mattoon's law," Peter shouted. "How come the high and mighty have got the laws on their side and the plain man hasn't got any on his? Who makes the laws?"

"The General Court—"

"The General Robbers. The General Lawyers. The General Liars and Cheaters." He spit. "No, sir, Porter, you're not taking my oxen. I'm warning you. Untie them and get off my farm."

"Peter," Molly said sharply.

I was kind of scared. When Peter lost his temper, he was likely to do almost anything.

"Now, Peter," the sheriff said calmly, "you prevent me today, and they'll just send four of us up here tomorrow to pick up the oxen and maybe take you along as well for interfering with the law. There's no use in it."

Peter grabbed his arm again. "I'm warning you."

"Let go of me, Peter."

"By God, I'm warning you, Porter."

"Peter," Molly shouted. He swiveled his head around, and at that moment the sheriff did a little side skip and broke loose from Peter. He swung up on the horse, jerked the musket from its boot, and leveled it at Peter. Peter stood crouched, his arms at his side, about to charge.

Molly raced out of the doorway. "Justin," she shouted at me, "take the baby." I grabbed it out of her arms. She leaped up on Peter's back and grabbed him around his head, covering his eyes with her hands so he couldn't see. He staggered forward from the sudden weight, then righted himself.

"Get off, Molly."

"You just calm down, first," she said. He grabbed her hands with his, unpeeled them from his face, and shook her off. She jumped around in front of him. "Calm down," she said.

He stood staring at her, panting. Porter still had the musket leveled. He looked at the gun and then at Molly. Finally he said, "You'd better learn which side you're on, Porter, ours or theirs. We're not going to stand for it much longer. There's trouble coming and it'll be coming soon." Then he spit again, and walked off full speed toward the woodlot. I snatched up the saw from the side of the barn where I'd left it, and ran after him with it.

"Peter, I brought the saw in," He turned and stared at me. Then he took the saw and, without saying a word, turned around again and walked away. I knew he was going to work off his temper cutting wood.

This was in a town called Pelham, in the western part of Massachusetts. Peter's farm is on East Hill, about nine miles east of the Connecticut River. Molly is my sister. My mother and father are dead. My father got killed in the Revolution. My mother was always sickly, and trying to run the farm without my father was hard on her. Especially with only two kids to help her. When she died, Molly and I moved in with my Uncle Billy. His name is Conkey, same as mine, and he owns a little tavern a couple of miles down the road. I kind of liked working at the tavern. But then Peter McColloch came home from the Revolution. Being as he was a hero, Molly fell in love with him, and they got married and bought this farm. Then, after the little ones started to be born, they needed help on the farm, so I came out here to live. I liked it. It was hard work, but Peter made it fun.

You never knew what Peter was likely to do. If he decided to do something, he'd go right ahead and do it. I mean, for example, once he was down at Uncle Billy's tavern drinking cider brandy with some of his friends and a peddler came in with a lot of thread and buttons and ornaments. Well, the peddler had a set of silver buttons that struck Peter's fancy. He said that they were pretty enough to be on Molly's best dress. The price was ten shillings, and my Uncle Billy Conkey said he shouldn't buy them—ten shillings was a lot of money and he couldn't afford it. But Peter didn't pay any attention to what Uncle Billy said, he just pulled the money out of his purse and gave it to the man, then he went on home and gave the buttons to Molly. Well, of course she was surprised and happy, but when she found out what they'd cost she hit the ceiling. It was too late to take them back, though—the peddler had already gone. That's the way Peter was. He was always doing something on the spur of the moment.

Of course, he lost his temper on the spur of the moment a lot, too. That part of it was bad, because sometimes he got into trouble for swearing at somebody, or even getting into a fight. But he was just as likely to do something nice as lose his temper. I mean, if I happened to be down in Amherst with him and we went by Kellogg's store where there was some candy or something in the window, he was likely to say, "How would you like some of that candy, Justin?" and take me in and buy it for me. So you can see, even if he flared up at me sometimes, he was fun, too.

One reason why Peter flared up so quickly was because he was big and brave and not afraid of anybody. He was a hero in the Revolution. He was in Major William Hull's Fourth Regiment, which was part of Anthony Wayne's Brigade. Once, during the Battle of Stony Point, a British squad had built a parapet on top of a hill where they could shoot down at the Americans at the bottom of the hill in perfect safety. The Americans were completely pinned down. So Major Hull called for volunteers for a "Forlorn Hope Squad." They were supposed to charge up the hill, leap over the parapet, and drive the British out with their bayonets. He promised three hundred dollars to the first man over the parapet, two hundred dollars to the next, and one hundred to the rest.

The way Peter told the story was, "Well, I'd raced everybody in my company one time or another, and I knew there wasn't anybody around who could run faster than me, because I'd beat them all. I figured if I volunteered, that three hundred dollars was as good as mine. So I said I'd go, and then one runty little follow, he said, 'McColloch, you may run faster than me, but big as you are you're bound to catch a ball before you get halfway up that hill and I'll beat you anyway.' So he volunteered and then a few others came in, and off we went. We just charged out from the trees where we were hiding with our bayonets fixed, shouting and hollering and calling the lobsterbacks names. And of course, I jumped out into the lead right away.

"Well, I hadn't gone more than about fifty yards when something occurred to me that I ought to have thought about earlier, which was that being so big and out front like that I was drawing all the British fire to myself and the other men weren't getting any. Those balls were whizzing by me pretty good, a couple of them so close I could feel the breeze they left. So I began to zigzag a little, first running to one side and then to the other side. Still those balls were hitting all around me. Some of them you could actually see skip off the ground, throwing up a little puff of dirt as they hit. So then another thing occurred to me, which was that the British weren't much good at shooting, and if I went on zigzagging I'd be just as likely to get hit by a bad shot as a good one. I decided I'd best put my trust in the bad aim of the British and get on up that hill as fast as I could. So I left off zigzagging and went on up the hill in a straight line, with the rest of the fellows strung out behind me.

"As I began to close in, I could see the British behind the parapet beginning to get kind of frantic, firing and reloading hardly without even pointing in the right direction. About this time I got to within ten yards of the parapet and I let out a big whoop and raised myself up to look as big and ferocious as I could. Then I leaped onto the parapet and took a slash at the first Britisher I could see. There wasn't any use in it, though, for they were all running down the other side of the hill, and I just dropped over the parapet and lay there laughing and shaking and feeling weak all over and just about as surprised as I could be that I was still alive."

That was the kind of man he was. It explains why he came so close to hitting Sheriff Porter. Most other men would have ranted and raged, but they wouldn't have hit a sheriff. But Peter would have if Molly hadn't stopped him. He wasn't afraid of anybody. He was a real hero, and I admired him so. The one thing I wanted, more than anything, was to do something glorious and brave so that Peter would admire me, too. But my life was just ordinary, and there was never anything glorious and brave to do.

Peter had been lucky. He'd been able to get into the Revolutionary War. But that war was over when I was just a little boy, and it didn't look as if there were going to be any more wars. I was sorry about that. How could I ever do something brave if there wasn't war? Oh, there probably would be more Indian wars out West, but there weren't many Indians around our part of the country now, and the ones that were here were pretty tame anyway.

I watched the sheriff lead the oxen out of the yard, and then I went inside. Molly and Peter's house had a main room with a big fireplace where they cooked, and a bedroom next to that, and upstairs two little rooms under the eaves. The baby slept with them, and the two other little ones in one of the upstairs rooms, and I had the other bedroom. There wasn't much to my room—just a rope bed with a straw mattress, a little table for my candle, and a chest where I kept my things. I don't have much to keep, except our family Bible, my father's will, and a sword my father got from General Lincoln for bravery at the Battle of Bennington. I tried to keep the sword polished so it wouldn't get rusty.

By the time Peter finished up in the woodlot and came down to milk the cow, the sun had gotten over to the tree line at the far end of the farm. It was getting dark inside, but Molly hadn't lit any candles yet. There was a big table in the middle of the main room, and four chairs, and two cupboards and a couple of chests for storing flour and so forth. Molly was sitting at the table with the little ones around her. They were upset. The baby was crying and the other two were looking worried. Molly was dipping bits of bread in apple molasses and feeding it to them to cheer them up. They stuffed it in their mouths and the molasses ran down their chins.

I sat down at the table and she sat down across from me, holding the baby on her lap where she could wipe its chin. "I didn't know Peter owed Major Mattoon money," I said.

"He had to borrow on the oxen to pay the taxes last year."

"How much was it?"

"Forty shillings."

"I didn't know that," I said.

"Everybody owes money. Everybody through this whole part of the state owes money."

It seemed like that was true. For the past few years, ever since the war stopped, all you ever heard about was debts and taxes and people going to court and paying huge lawyer fees. "Well, I don't understand it," I said.

"It's hard to understand," she said. "It's hard to understand why we have to struggle so, and lose our oxen, and those like Mattoon have all the money and great houses and don't have to dirty their hands working from one year to the next."

"With all he's got, why would he want to take Peter's oxen? What can it mean to him?"

"That's the way those people think," she said. "They think they're lords and masters of everything. They think they're the high and mighty and we're nothing. They don't care about people at all, it seems—only about things. Having more and more things—getting richer and richer."

I felt pretty sunk. It was hard enough running the farm as it was. Peter had only thirty acres. That was a pretty small farm, so we had to use every inch of it. That meant plowing some awfully stony fields. Without oxen there was no way to do it. Even if we could borrow a team of oxen from somebody for the plowing, that was only the beginning. What about hauling firewood up from the woodlot? We'd have to carry that on our backs, tons and tons of it.

Or bringing our flax down to Amherst—we'd have to put that up in fifty-pound bundles and walk nine miles with it on our backs. And if we cut up some oak planking to sell, the way Peter did in the winters, we'd have to carry the planks to whoever bought them on our shoulders one at a time. Leastwise, I'd have to carry them one at a time. Peter could easily take two and maybe three. It looked to me like the end of the oxen was the end of the farm.

At dusk Peter came in from the cowshed. He was still angry at Sheriff Porter and Major Mattoon, but he'd worked some of his anger off. "That's one thing about getting into a temper," he said. "It gets a lot of wood cut."

We sat down to supper—milk, johnnycake, cheese, and boiled eggs. Molly waited until Peter had stoked up a little bit. "What are you going to do about the oxen?" she said.

"Shoot somebody," he said.

"Peter," Molly said sharply. "I don't want any of that talk, even in jest."

"I'm not joking," he said. "I fought one war, I can fight another."

"Stop it," she said. "You'll scare the little ones."

He looked at the children. "You're not scared, are you?"

They shook their heads. I could see that they were scared, though. "Peter," I said, "I don't see how we can run the farm without the oxen."

"I know," he said. "We're going to get them back."

"How?"

"We're going over to see Daniel Shays," he said. "Maybe he and I'll shoot somebody together."

Chapter Two

I GUESS DANIEL SHAYS WAS THE MOST important man around Pelham. People knew about him from other towns, too. He'd fought in the Revolution at Lexington and Concord and Bunker Hill. He was at Stony Point with Peter, and because of his bravery at some other battles, General Lafayette gave him a fancy sword. But, smart and brave as he was, he was just as poor as any farmer around town— he'd even had to sell the Lafayette sword to pay his taxes.

Everybody called him Captain Shays, because he was captain of our militia. Every town had its militia. They drilled once a month on a Saturday afternoon. They were supposed to be ready to fight in case the British attacked again or there was an Indian uprising, which wasn't too likely in Massachusetts but happened farther west. The Massachusetts government could call up the militia whenever it wanted, and the men would have to go. Captain Shays' farm was next over from Uncle Billy's tavern. That was why we knew him so well. I was proud of knowing him, and when I used to work at the tavern I loved to watch him up on his horse, drilling the men and shouting out orders.

Peter and I rode over after supper. It was only about two miles over to where Captain Shays' house and the tavern was. It didn't take us long to get there. Captain Shays' house wasn't much bigger than ours. He was a plain farmer like the rest of us, except, of course, he was important. When we came in, he was sitting in his kitchen in front of the fire with his eyeglasses on, reading the *Hampshire Gazette*.

He put down the paper and got up. "Hello, Peter," he said. "Hello, Justin."

"Daniel, Porter took my oxen."

"I know," Captain Shays said quietly. "I heard he was coming after them. I hope you didn't make trouble."

"I pretty near did. Molly stopped me."

"That was sensible."

"Sensible," Peter said. "How am I going to do my plowing? I can't hook Justin to the plow, can I?"

"Sit down, Peter," Captain Shays said. "We'll have a mug of ale and talk it over calmly."

He got three wooden mugs and a pitcher of ale, and we sat down at the kitchen table before the fire. It was cozy sitting there drinking the ale, and it made me feel proud to be in on the men's conversation.

"I'm not feeling very calm," Peter said.

Captain Shays stared at Peter over his eyeglasses. "Peter, I've never seen you when you felt calm."

"That's so," Peter said. "But this time I have reason."

"You're not alone. There are thousands around this whole part of the state who are in your position. There's absolutely no good in your threatening to punch Sheriff Porter. It's time for concerted action."

I knew it wasn't my place to interrupt, but Captain Shays always seemed so friendly that I did it anyway. "Sir, what I don't understand is how everybody could be poor all at once. I mean, you could understand if some people were poor, but not everybody at the same time."

Peter scowled at me. "It's complicated, Just."

"No, no," Captain Shays said. "He should understand. He'll be a man shortly. The more the plain people understand what's happening to them, the better they'll be able to rectify the situation."

"Umph," Peter said, and took a drink of ale.

"Justin, it's true that it's complicated," Captain Shays said. "I'll try to make it simple. During the War for Independence, the government just didn't have enough money to buy supplies and pay the soldiers—not the Continental Congress, not the Massachusetts General Court. So they printed up paper money and tried to get rich Patriots to lend them specie."

"What's specie?" I asked. I could see this was going to be complicated all right.

"It's gold and silver coin," Peter said. "There's no reason you should know—there's never been any around our place." Just talking about it made Peter angry.

"Anyway," Captain Shays went on, "with all that paper money around and all the states just cranking it out as fast as the printing presses would turn, pretty soon it just wasn't worth anything so it got discounted." This time I didn't have to ask. Peter knew I wouldn't understand that.

"That means that a ten-dollar bill might pass for only five

dollars—or two dollars—or like the hundred-dollar Continental bills I got for risking my neck at Stony Point—they're only worth about two dollars each now. I was lucky. I got seven each." And then he laughed a sort of hollow make-believe laugh.

"You mean you got only twenty-one dollars instead of three hundred." I added fast.

"Yes, Justin," Captain Shays broke in, "and then Mattoon—"

"Mattoon," I gasped, "how'd he get them?"

"Mattoon was tax collector," Captain Shays said. "He paid the taxes himself in specie—just a few shillings—and kept the Continental dollars which he turned in for Massachusetts consolidated notes. Now those notes carry interest—six dollars on the hundred. And that's what the General Court is taxing us to pay."

"Yes, by God!" shouted Peter. "And a couple of years ago when I didn't have the money to pay my taxes so that the government could give Mattoon and the other high-and-mighties interest on my own money that Mattoon's got—that snake paid them for me. And now he's got my oxen." He banged his fist down on the table top so hard that it made the mugs jump.

"But that's so unfair," I shouted. "Doesn't the government see how unfair it is?"

The men were silent. Finally Captain Shays said, "I don't know if they see it. The government isn't a thing—it's people. And just now it's mostly Mattoon's kind of people. Anyway, they're way off in Boston. I don't think they have much idea of how people around here are suffering. Peter isn't the only one in trouble."

"It's the same everywhere, Justin," Peter said. "Everywhere people are being taxed to death, everywhere people are losing their oxen, their cattle, their flax, sometimes even their farms. And if they haven't got anything left to take, then the government puts them in debtors' prison until somebody pays their debts for them. And on top of it there's the lawyers."

"That's almost the worst of it," Captain Shays said. "The court fees are so high that even if a plain man wins his case, it'll leave him in debt to the lawyers. The lawyers aren't plain men like us. The lawyers are in cahoots with the speculators, the rich. The lawyers and the speculators are the ones who run the government these days. The lawyers get to be the judges. They don't have much idea of lowering court fees."

"I thought we could vote in whoever we wanted. Why do we have to have only the rich folks running the government?"

Peter didn't say anything. Captain Shays took off his eyeglasses and began swinging them around by the earpiece. "Unfortunately, Justin, a lot of towns in this part of the state didn't send representatives to our legislature, the General Court."

"But why not?"

"Too expensive. The people would have to tax themselves to pay the salaries and expenses of their representatives. They didn't think it was worth it. A lot of people figured that the government was way over in Boston and it didn't have any interest in us, anyway. It was a mistake, we know that now. But it's too late to change that until the next election, in April."

Peter smacked his fist down on the table again. "But meanwhile what are we going to do? How can we safeguard our little bits of property?"

"We have to work together, Peter. That's why there's no point in your going off half-cocked. There are some ideas going around. People are beginning to talk about this plan or that plan. I think things will happen."

"What?"

"Closing the courts, for one. The judges travel from one town to the next, hearing cases. They may get to this part of the state every two or three months."

"Yes?" Peter said.

"Well, look, Peter, let's say for the sake of argument you owed Major Mattoon forty shillings. And let's say he decided to take your oxen to settle the debt. After all, a good team of oxen is worth about six times that. He can take your oxen because he's a justice of the peace, but he can't auction them off without an order from a higher court. So he waits until the court comes to Northampton the next time, and gets ready to go in with his papers. But then suppose the night before the court was to meet, a body of armed men came down into Northampton. And suppose that the next morning when the judges came to the courthouse they found it surrounded by these men. And suppose these men then politely suggest to the judges that they go away without holding court."

Peter was grinning. "Then Mattoon couldn't get his court order. He couldn't sell my oxen."

"Now, Peter, let me say—" He stopped and looked at me. "Justin, you must swear never to mention to anybody what I'm saying."

"Yes, sir," I said. "I swear it."

"It's important. Lives may depend on it."

"I swear, sir."

He nodded. "All right. Now, Peter, there is a court meeting in Northampton next week. That is where all the creditors will get their writs to take our property. Mattoon is a justice of the peace, and you can bet he'll give writs to anyone who asks, because he's going to issue plenty of his own—he'll be both plaintiff and judge in his own case. But it wouldn't surprise me in the least if there were a party of armed men there at the same time to see that they don't meet. I was hoping you might be one of them."

Peter smacked his hand down on the table and gave a big laugh. "By God, Daniel, I'll be there."

"I kind of thought you would."

"I'm going, too," I said suddenly.

Peter stared at me. "No, you're not," he said. "There might be fighting."

It was a chance to do something brave and glorious. Maybe my last chance. "I want to go, too, Peter."

"No. That's that."

"Why not?"

"Because there might be fighting. I don't want you getting hurt."

"If you can take a chance on getting hurt, why can't I?"

His hand smacked down on the table one more time and the mugs jumped. "No. That's final."

I knew better than to say anything.

Suddenly Peter frowned. "But what about my oxen? Stopping the courts won't help any. Mattoon's already got his court order and taken them."

Captain Shays started swinging his eyeglasses again, looking up at the ceiling. "Well, Peter, I had a thought about that," he said.

"Yes?"

"It occurred to me that Justin might go into service with Major Mattoon to earn the oxen back."

"Never," Peter said. "I'm not having any member of my family becoming a servant. We're free men."

"Hold on a little, Peter. How much was the debt? Forty shillings?"

"I won't have Justin in Mattoon's house."

"Forty shillings, Peter?"

Peter nodded. "Forty shillings."

"Figure three shillings a week and board as wages for a boy. He'd have it paid up before Christmas. In exchange for his services he'd let you have your oxen back now, in time for fall plowing."

Peter frowned, considering. "No," he said finally. "I don't want Justin to be anybody's servant. Especially Mattoon's."

"Peter," Captain Shays said. "Listen to me, Peter. I'm not just thinking about your oxen. I'm also thinking about how useful it would be for us to have somebody in Major Mattoon's household who was on our side. A smart young fellow like Justin might overhear things. He might see people coming and going. He might find a scrap of paper with some useful information on it. He might even put his ear to a wall, his eye to a keyhole."

They were both staring at me. My heart was pounding in my chest. It was my chance to do something glorious.

"I think you get the idea, Peter," Captain Shays said.

Chapter Three

MAJOR MATTOON WAS RICH. HE'D BEEN TO Dartmouth College and I guess he knew a lot of things that most people didn't. One thing he knew was how to make money. And he was always busy. He bought things like cheese and cider brandy and oats and corn from the farmers around. Sometimes he sent what he bought to Boston by wagon to be sold there, sometimes he shipped things down the Connecticut River to Hartford or even New York. He bought a lot of flax, too, which was made into linen. Some of the flax he bought was shipped as far as Ireland, to be made into fine Irish linen. We grew flax like a lot of the farmers. Molly spun it into yarn and sold it to Major Mattoon.

He was also in the land speculation business. He would buy land from people cheap and sell it when the price went up. Because so many people in our part of Massachusetts were in debt, he could often pick up land cheap. Or maybe there would be some new land opened up someplace farther west from us, like New York State. Such land always sold very cheap, and Major Mattoon would buy some of it and hold onto it until they got the Indians out of the area and it got more settled, which would make the price of the land go up. He wasn't the only rich man around. There were others, mostly along the Connecticut River where the best soil was. Everybody called them the River Gods.

Most of the plain farmers lived in wooden houses, but Major Mattoon had a big brick house with a wall around it. To get to it you went through a gate and down a long lane lined with maple trees. There was grass all around the house, and off to one side a big barn, storehouses, and such. From a hill back of the barn you could see the Connecticut River, and beyond the barn, his fields of corn and wheat and oats.

Peter and I rode down Major Mattoon's lane on Peter's horse, Brother. Peter was mighty proud of that horse because it had a very steady gait. He said that Brother could carry a glass of water on his back without spilling a drop. We rode around to the back of the house. Plain people like Peter and me wouldn't come in the front door, but through the back, where the kitchen and washrooms were. We went into the kitchen. There was a cook there kneading dough, and a man polishing silver. The man looked at us when we came in. "Yes," he said sharply.

"I'm Peter McColloch. I want to see Major Mattoon."

"He's busy. What do you want to see him about?"

Peter stared at the man. "What business is it of yours?"

"I'm Major Mattoon's groom. He doesn't see everybody who walks in the back door."

"Then I'll go around to the front door," Peter said.

The cook had stopped kneading the dough to watch the argument. "Peter," I said, "don't lose your temper."

He took a deep breath. "I have business with Major Mattoon."

"What kind of business? He doesn't see every—"

"Damn." Peter smacked a fist into the palm of his other hand. "Just tell him Peter McColloch is here."

The groom was looking nervous. "It'd better be something worth bothering the major for," he said. He went out of the room, and came back in five minutes. "You can see him," he said. We followed the groom out of the kitchen, through the dining room, and down a hall. There was a lot of curved furniture everywhere, and on the wall big paintings of river scenes and portraits of people in fancy clothes.

At the end of the hall was a door. The groom pushed it open, and then gestured for us to go in. Major Mattoon was sitting at a large desk. There were books around the walls and behind him a cabinet of narrow drawers where he kept his papers. He was reading something, and we stood in front of the desk waiting until he had finished. Finally he dropped the paper onto a stack of others and looked up. For a moment he stared at us, first Peter, then me, and then Peter again. I was surprised at how young he looked. He wasn't much older than Peter, around thirty-two, I'd judge. I figured he must be pretty smart to get rich that young.

"McColloch," he said. "Peter McColloch. It's the oxen, I suppose."

"Yes, sir," Peter said. I knew he was going to try to be polite. "It's a great loss to us."

"I expect it must be," Major Mattoon said. "I'm sorry to have to take them. You know, I work just as hard at my business as you do at yours. I'd much rather have had my money."

"I would rather you had it, too, sir. We can't plow without oxen. If you gave us another few weeks, maybe I could find the money some way."

"McColloch, you know and I know that there isn't any way you can raise forty shillings in a few months, much less a few weeks. I'm sorry, but as you no doubt remember, I extended the loan twice."

"I know that, sir. I was hoping you'd give me one more chance."

He leaned back in his chair with his hands behind his head. "McColloch, let me give you a little lesson in finance, which nobody around this part of the state seems to understand. Every time a farmer around here gets into trouble, the first thing he thinks of is Major Mattoon. Surely kindhearted Major Mattoon, with his vast holdings, will be able to spare the small matter of forty shillings. Why for a man of his great wealth, he wouldn't even notice the loss of forty shillings. So down he comes, all humble and smiling, telling me what a kind gentleman I am and how much I am admired through the countryside."

"Sir—" Peter said. I doubted that he'd ever told Major Mattoon what a kind gentleman he was.

Major Mattoon held up his hand. "One moment, McColloch. So where am I left? I turn the man down, I am a cold, unfeeling brute. If I out and out make him a present of the money, which I am willing to admit I could easily afford to do, by the end of the day there will be twenty more at my doorstep and by the end of the week a hundred, all with their hands out, and a year later my house and my lands would be sold up and I would be in debtors' prison myself. So what do I do? I *lend* him the money. And then he can't repay. So I give him six months. And still he can't repay. So I give him three months more, and then another three months. But in the end, I must have something for my money. And I take the oxen."

It was hard to argue against that. You couldn't expect him to give all his money away. Still, it seemed awfully unfair for him to have this great house and barns and fields and men working for him, and to take our oxen, too.

"Major Mattoon, I can't run the farm without the oxen."

"I wish there were something I could do, McColloch. I'm not hard-hearted. But I must have something for my money."

"Major Mattoon," I said, "I'll come to work for you."

He shifted his eyes to look at me instead of Peter. "Come to work for me?"

"If you let Peter take the oxen back, I'll come down and work for you until the forty shillings are paid back."

"It's a little more than forty shillings. There was interest on it."

He didn't say anything for a minute. Then he looked back at Peter. "This is your brother?"

"My brother-in-law. My wife's brother."

"You'd put him into service to pay up your debt?"

Peter flushed and his jaw jutted forward. "I don't have much choice, do I?"

"What can he do?"

"He's a good, strong boy. He's worked the farm with me, and he's worked over at Conkey's tavern. Billy Conkey is his uncle."

"The tavern," Major Mattoon said. "Then he's used to sweeping and polishing and cleaning."

"Yes, sir," I said. "I can do all that. I used to keep the tavern clean."

Major Mattoon nodded. "Jasper's been complaining about being overworked. He could use some help."

"Jasper?"

"The groom." He drummed on the desk. He picked up a pen and began to figure on a piece of paper. "Let's make it two shillings a week, and board. The sum is forty shillings, with interest for two years compounded comes to forty-four shillings, twelve pence. It makes twenty-two weeks' work."

My heart sank. That was nearly half a year.

"Major Mattoon, two shillings a week isn't very much for a good boy."

"McColloch, I am not a charitable institution," he said sharply. "Take it or leave it."

So that was how I came to work for Major Mattoon. We took the oxen back that afternoon, and the next day Peter rode me down on Brother with my clothes. "Keep your eyes open," he told me at the door. "I'll get down as often as I can to see you." It made me forlorn to see him ride away. I was now living among strangers.

Jasper showed me my room, a little sort of cubbyhole up in the top of the house big enough for a rope bed and a little chest for my clothes. It didn't matter much—I wasn't there very often. I had to get up at five o'clock every morning to get fires going if we needed them, and help the cook get the family's breakfast started. Jasper got up at six and set the table with white cloths, polished silver, and gleaming glassware. There were six of them in the family—Major Mattoon, Mrs. Mattoon, their two children, who were six and eight, Major Mattoon's old aunt, and some girl who was a cousin. They had ten servants to take care of them. There were six people who worked his farms—the home-farm by the house where they grew food for the house, and the out-farm where they grew mostly corn and flax for the market. At the home-farm we had four cows, swine, sheep, and pretty near two acres of kitchen garden, and a little herb garden that the cook tended, and an orchard with apple and pear trees. Then there was a house maid, a seamstress who made the clothes for the family, and a cook. And, of course, Jasper, who waited on table and drove the coach, and me.

I was houseboy. It was my job to bring up wood and do the heavy cleaning, like scrubbing floors, washing windows, polishing the brass hinges, door knobs, fire screens, and such like. I worked right through until after the family had finished supper, when I helped Jasper clean up the dining room. Then I had my own supper. Sometimes I'd try to sit before the kitchen fire and read, but mostly I'd be too tired and I'd fall asleep in my chair before I'd read two pages. I hated it. The work was so boring, and I hated taking orders from Jasper or even Major Mattoon. One thing about it was how Major Mattoon treated everybody who worked for him. He just snapped out an order as if I were a dog. He was as polite and nice as could be to his

friends, rich people like himself. But he never said
"Please" or "Thank you" to us plain people, it was just "Do
this" and "Do that" and you were supposed to say, "Yes,
sir," and walk away and do it. And the way they ate. When
I thought about how hard Molly and Peter worked to put a
little johnnycake and syrup on the table while Mrs. Mattoon didn't seem to do much more than a little nee-
dlework, but got served fancy food every evening, it made
me wonder. But there was nothing I could do about it. All
I could do was grit my teeth and keep my eyes open.

The main thing was to learn how things worked in the
household. I had one big advantage as a spy: The kind of
job I had let me go around the house pretty free. I mean,
being as I was supposed to keep the brass polished, I had
plenty of chances to go into Major Mattoon's library and
have a look around. There were sometimes papers lying on
his desk, although mostly he kept them locked up in the
cabinet behind the desk. I'd try to get in the library every
couple of days or so when Major Mattoon happened to
leave the door unlocked, and sneak a look at any papers I
could find. Most of them were about business and didn't
interest me very much, but I kept on looking. You never
knew what might turn up.

Then, one day, two weeks after I'd started working
there, a man came galloping up to the front door, dashed
into the house, and ran down to Major Mattoon's library.
A few minutes later, Major Mattoon and the man came
running out of the library. Major Mattoon was shouting,
"Jasper, Jasper, saddle Columbia. Quickly, quickly." Jasper
was in the pantry, polishing silver. He dropped the teapot
he was working on back onto the table and raced out of the

house as fast as I'd ever seen him run. And in five minutes Major Mattoon and the other man were gone.

When Jasper came back, I went into the pantry. "What was it, Jasper?"

"I don't know," he said abruptly. "And I wouldn't tell you if I did know. It's none of your business."

But that evening I took some cider out to the men working in the barn. One of them had been into the village to pick up a barrel of nails Major Mattoon had ordered, and he'd got the story from some people at a tavern he'd stopped into. "A bunch of men marched into Springfield and stopped the court there," he was telling the rest. I stood and listened. "Oh, there were maybe a thousand of them. They wouldn't let the judges into the courthouse, and finally the judges left."

"That's revolution," one man said.

"Don't know what you call it," the other said, "but it's time the people stood up for their rights."

"Don't expect it's going to agree with Major Mattoon very well."

My heart lifted. Captain Shays had done it. Oh, how I envied Peter. I'd have given anything to have been in on it. But now I knew that I should stick as close to Major Mattoon as I possibly could. It was my job to find out what he and the other rich men around were planning to do in return.

Chapter Four

MAJOR MATTOON CAME BACK IN THE EVENING three days later. He rode up with the man he had left with, and they strode into the house looking tired and dirty and angry. "Jasper," he shouted. "Bring us some supper into the library. And some wine. Immediately."

They strode down the hall to the library, and of course Jasper began shouting for me. I went out into the kitchen. The cook was hastily slicing up some cold beef, which she put on a platter with some bread and eggs. "Conkey," Jasper said, "get two bottles of wine out of the cellar and take them in to the major. Quickly now."

I got the wine, napkins, two glasses, and the corkscrew, put them all on a silver tray the way Jasper had taught me, and went down the corridor to the library. The two men were sitting at the table across the room from Major Mattoon's desk. I put the tray down on a side table and began wiping the bottles clean with the napkin, going about as slow as I dared.

"It's just the beginning, Tyler," Major Mattoon said. "They'll do it again."

"I have no doubt of it, Major."

"It's treason, pure and simple. It's a hanging offense."

"Pretty hard to hang a thousand men," Mr. Tyler said.

Just then Jasper came in with the platter of food. He put it on the table between the two men and then began to serve each of them a plateful.

"Where's that wine, Conkey?" Major Mattoon said.

"Just coming, sir," I said. "The cork was pretty tight."

I pulled the cork, carried the bottle over to the table, filled the glasses, and went back to where I had left the other bottle. Jasper finished serving and left. As he went by me he said, "Be quick about it, Conkey." I picked up the other bottle and slowly began to wipe it clean.

"The point is that next time we must be better prepared," Mr. Tyler said.

"That's it indeed. How do we respond? What do we do?"

That was the important part; it was what I wanted to hear.

"I'd try to avoid a pitched battle. I don't know as we want to open fire on them," Mr. Tyler said.

"We might have to."

"Still, it's to be avoided if we can. Besides, will the militia fire if ordered to? It would mean shooting their own people."

"It might throw a scare into them," Major Mattoon said.

"What we really want are the leaders. If we could catch a few of them, the whole thing would dissolve without further trouble. These people need leaders."

Suddenly Major Mattoon noticed that I was still there. "Conkey, what the devil are you doing with that wine?"

"Opening this other bottle for you, sir."

"Must you be so slow about it?"

"I'm hurrying, sir." I put down the napkin and turned the corkscrew into the cork.

Mr. Tyler reached into his coat and took out a piece of paper. "I have a list of names, Major," he said. "I drew it up last night. I'm pretty sure these are some of the ringleaders."

He passed the paper over to Major Mattoon. The major read it down, frowning. I sure wanted to have a look at that piece of paper. It would be important for Captain Shays to know who they thought the leaders were.

Major Mattoon finished reading the paper. "That'll be very useful," he said. He folded it up, rose, and walked across the room to the cabinet behind his desk. "Conkey, haven't you finished yet? Leave us, we want to be alone."

"Yes, sir," I said. I pulled the cork, took the bottle over to where they were sitting, put it down on the table, and walked toward the door. I just had time to notice which drawer Major Mattoon put the list of names into before I went out.

Peter came down to see me two days later. Jasper wouldn't let him in the house, so we went out to the low shed where the firewood was kept, sat on the logs, and Peter told me about Springfield. "There wasn't anything to it," he said with a grin. "We marched down there and then marched up and down in front of the courthouse for a while. The militia under General Sheppard was there, but we didn't figure they'd shoot us. They're just plain people like ourselves, most of them are on our side anyway. Finally the judges gave in and left without holding court. Sheppard dismissed the militia and we all went home." He grinned again. "There was nothing to it," he said.

"Are you going to do it again?"

"In a couple of weeks there'll be a court in Worcester. I think Daniel Shays will want to do the same thing there."

"Is Captain Shays the leader?"

"Not exactly. There's several of them from various places who are leaders. Luke Day from West Springfield, Job Shattuck from Groton, Eli Parsons from over in Berkshire County—and there's others, too. But they all respect Daniel. They look to him for good advice."

"Peter, Major Mattoon has a list of the leaders in his cabinet."

"Are you sure?"

"Yes. He was discussing it with Mr. Tyler. They had the list, but I couldn't get a look at it."

"Where is it now?"

"Locked up in his cabinet."

"Do you think you can get it?"

"It would be pretty hard," I said. "But I could try."

"It would be mighty useful to know what they're thinking, Justin."

"I'll try, Peter."

It wasn't going to be easy. That evening Jasper had me bring Major Mattoon the glass of port he always had before going to bed. It gave me a chance to get a look at the cabinet. It was about six feet high and three or four feet wide. It had two doors that swung open. Inside, there were two rows of narrow drawers going all the way from top to bottom. There were little paper labels on each drawer, telling what was in each one. The doors weren't paneled like ordinary cabinet doors, but were solid oak, which was almost as hard as iron. Well, not that hard, but hard enough. You could cut through it with an ax, but it would take a while. If you hit a door made of pine with an ax it would split on the first blow. You could bust through even hard maple with a couple of swings. But it might take ten minutes to smash open an oak door with an ax. And, of course, it would make an awful noise and bring everybody running.

It would be a better idea to try to pry the doors open. The lock was set in the middle of the righthand door. I figured that if I could get something in the crack between the doors I might be able to spread the doors enough so that the lock would pull apart. You could do that sometimes.

But was the crack wide enough? I wasn't sure. Was there any way I could get the key? That didn't seem very likely. Major Mattoon surely had some hiding place for his keys. Besides that, he usually locked up the library when he went away. But maybe there was some way to get hold of the key to the cabinet doors. I mean, if he went out for a minute while the key was in the door, maybe I could quickly steal it. Suppose I came rushing in and said that one of the men had got kicked by a horse, or that there was a fire in the barn; he might rush out without thinking about the key, and I could snatch it up. Or maybe even have time to search through the cabinet for my papers. But then, of course, he'd go outside and find out that nobody had got hurt, or that there wasn't any fire, and he'd probably have me arrested and put in jail for lying.

There wasn't any easy answer. Over the next week or so I went on puzzling over it. Whenever I got a chance to come into the library, I tried to get as close as I could to the cabinet to examine it more carefully, but I never had enough time to get a real look at it. Major Mattoon was always there. I had to admit he really did work pretty hard.

Meanwhile, Major Mattoon had put me to work oiling the floors. It was nasty, dirty work, which I had to fit into my regular chores. I hated doing it. And I was doing this one morning when it happened all over again—Mr. Tyler came tearing up on his horse, Major Mattoon began shouting for Jasper to saddle Columbia, and a few minutes later the two men dashed away. I grinned where nobody could see me, because I knew that Daniel Shays and Peter and the rest of them were out closing another court.

Major Mattoon was going to be gone for two or three days. Nobody else in the house knew it, but because of what Peter had told me, I did. It was an ideal time for me to get a good look at the cabinet. But how? The library door would be locked, of course. I wondered if Jasper had a key to it. He had a big ring of keys he carried around on his belt, but I didn't know what the keys were for.

I went on oiling the floors, and in the middle of the afternoon I ran out of oil. I went out into the pantry where Jasper was polishing silver.

"I'm out of oil, Jasper," I said.

"I'm busy. I can't get it for you now."

"Major Mattoon told me to oil the floors. How am I supposed to do it if I don't have any oil?"

"You should have thought of it before."

"I'll get it myself." The oil was locked up in the paint closet in the cellar, along with a lot of other things like wax, polish, and so forth. "Just give me the key, and I'll get it myself."

"Nobody's supposed to touch these keys but me. Major Mattoon doesn't trust anybody but me with them."

"Come on, Jasper. What am I going to do, steal a bucket

of paint?"

"There's no telling what you'd do, Justin. You're getting too big for your britches." But he undid his belt and slid the key ring off. It was a big iron ring about four inches in diameter. There were ten or fifteen keys on it. It weighed nearly two pounds. It must have been a big nuisance carrying it around all the time, but I guessed it made Jasper proud to have them. "It's this one," he said. "Get your oil and bring the keys back immediately."

I went out of the pantry and into the kitchen where the cellar door was. The cook was kneading dough. I went right on through the kitchen, and as soon as I was out of sight of the cook I began to run down the long hall to the library. I was there in ten seconds. Nobody was around. The library doors were shut. I began trying the keys in the library door lock, one at a time. The fifth one went smoothly in. My heart was beating so I could hear it throbbing in my chest. I turned the key gently, and pushed the door open. Then I slipped across the room to the cabinet. Again I tried the keys. None fit. Major Mattoon may have trusted Jasper with the keys to the paint closet, but he didn't trust him with the key to his papers.

Now I began to study the cabinet. I saw right away that the crack between the doors was pretty fine. You could probably pound a chisel into it, and then maybe pry the doors apart, but you'd make a lot of noise doing it. Next I checked the hinges. They were set in the jamb—there was no way I could get them. It was worrisome. I stepped back and looked the whole thing over again. There was a large brass plate over the keyhole, and one matching it on the other door. The plate would have been put on to cover the rough hole they made for the lock in the wood underneath.

The plate was held down by screws. It would be possible to unscrew them and take the plate off. Once it was off I might some way be able to get at the lock. But how?

I didn't have any more time to worry about it, though. Quickly I turned, went out of the library, shut the doors, and locked them. Then I snapped open Jasper's key ring, took the library key off it, stuck it in my pocket, and closed the key ring again. I dashed down the hall, into the kitchen, and down the cellar stairs. Quickly I opened the paint closet, grabbed out the oil jar, and came back up. Jasper gave me a look when I came into the pantry. "Here are the keys," I said.

"What took you so long?"

"I forgot which was the right key. I had to try them all."

He undid his belt, slipped the key ring over it, and did it up again. "If you paid attention to your work instead of daydreaming all the time, you might not have Major Mattoon on your back all the time."

I didn't say anything, but took the oil and went back out to oil the hall floor.

By the middle of the afternoon, word was beginning to go around that Captain Shays and his men were trying to close another court. The servants began to realize that their master would be gone at least overnight, and maybe for two or three days, and they began to take little holidays for themselves. The farmers drew lots to see who would stay around to look after things and the winners all went off into Amherst to stand around the taverns and drink. Jasper and the maid went off somewhere—out in the cornfield, I figured.

I hung around the pantry until they were gone. Then I stole a half-dozen candles out of the candle box and wrapped them up in a napkin. Next I went out to the barn, where they kept the tools. The tools were supposed to be locked up when nobody was using them, but I figured they wouldn't be, and I was right. The tool chest was standing open. I took out a screwdriver, a couple of small chisels, and a file. I wrapped these up in the dust cloth along with the candles. I went across the yard to the woodshed, slipped into the back, and tucked the whole package deep down inside the woodpile. Then I went back into the house. I was feeling scared all right, but pretty good, too. I thought my plan might work.

Then there was nothing to do but wait it out until it was night. I helped Jasper serve the family supper. When we got finished, he went off with the maid and I went upstairs to my room so people would think I'd gone to bed. After a little while I began to hear distant voices coming from the kitchen. The servants were having a little party. I figured that they'd probably opened up a few bottles of Major Mattóon's wine and were getting drunk. That was so much the better—they'd be less likely to worry about where I was.

The big clock in the hall below struck ten. I went on lying on my bed. I was pretty sleepy, and after a while I dozed off for a little. When I woke up it was after eleven. I got up and slipped downstairs barefoot. I went outside and across the yard to the woodshed. I climbed up on the woodpile, got my package out, and then stood for a moment looking at the house. There was a light on in the upstairs, the old aunt's room. That didn't mean anything: She usually kept a candle burning through the night so she could see in case she had to get up. The family was asleep.

Most of the rest of the house was dark, too, except the

kitchen. I slipped across the yard to the house and crept up to the kitchen window.

The cook was there, and Jasper and the maid, and a couple of the farmers. The maid was sitting on Jasper's lap. There were some open wine bottles on the kitchen table, and a jug of cider. They were laughing and shouting. I figured they were pretty drunk.

Now I turned back and went the other way along the house to where there was a side door letting into the hall. I opened it and slipped inside. The place was pitch dark. It didn't matter, I knew where everything was. I felt along in the dark, going slowly down the hall to the library. Fumbling with my hand I found the keyhole, slid the key in, and turned it. Then I went in and closed the doors behind me.

I knelt down in front of where I figured the cabinet was, unrolled my package on the floor, and felt around until I found one of the candles. I felt on the desk for the tinder-box I always used to light the fire, and turned the wheel against the flint. Almost immediately the old, dry tow cloth began to glow and then flame. I lit the candle. The library windows faced south, away from the kitchen. It wasn't likely that anybody would be out in that direction in the middle of the night. I stuck the candle in one of the holders on Major Mattoon's desk. Then I dumped everything off the cloth and spread it on the floor just in front of the cabinet. Next I picked up the screwdriver and began taking out the screws that held the brass plate over the lock. There were six of them, and it didn't take me more than a couple of minutes to do it. I laid the screws down carefully on Major Mattoon's desk where I could find them again. When I got the last one out, the plate came off as easy as pie. It was just as I had thought. Underneath the plate was a rough hole, about an inch across. Down inside the hole I could see the part of the steel lock that had the keyhole in it. The lock had been fitted into a neat hole cut in the edge of the door. The hole I was looking at had been cut in the side of the door so the key could pass through into the lock. I just hoped the lock wasn't too big.

Now I took the candle from Major Mattoon's desk, turned it sideways, and pushed the flame carefully up to the hole I had been studying. The trick was to get the flame as far into the hole as I could, without discouraging it too much. I got the hang of it after a minute. I kept turning the candle to make it burn evenly. Some of the wax dripped onto the door, but most of it fell down onto the cloth I had spread on the floor. I went on standing there, watching the flame. My heart was really thumping in my chest. I stood there like that for maybe five minutes. Then I saw a tiny glow. The wood was beginning to burn. I pulled the candle away. The glow went out. When I put the flame back against the wood, the glow reappeared. I went on working the candle around the hole, and after another five minutes or maybe more—I couldn't be sure how long it was—the edges of the hole all the way around were glowing. I kept on working for another little while. Then I pulled the candle away. The edge of the hole was charred all the way around. I put the candlestick on the cloth I had spread on the floor and stuck the candle in it. I picked up one of the little chisels. Working carefully so as not to make any noise, I scrapped off the charred edges around the hole. It only took a couple of minutes to get down to fresh wood. I put the chisel down, took the candle out of the candlestick, and once more set about charring the edges of the hole.

Time was passing. Every once in a while I could hear a faint laugh or whoop from the direction of the kitchen. I wondered what time it was. There was a grandfather clock out in the hall, but I didn't want to risk moving around any more than I had to. As close as I could figure, by the time I'd scraped off the charred edges of the hole the second time I'd been there a half an hour. I'd already started on the second candle.

But the hole was nearly twice as big now. If I could just stay patient, in time I'd have the whole lock uncovered. Then all I had to do was pry it out, and the cabinet door would swing open. The problem was keeping patient. I was as nervous as a treed cat. I kept having the impulse to just start hacking away at the wood around the lock to speed things up. But I kept myself under control, and went on burning and scraping, burning and scraping, and finally I had the wood cleared completely from the top edge of the lock. That cheered me up, because it gave me some idea of how big the lock was. I figured it couldn't be more than about two inches or so square. I went on burning and scraping, first along the top, and then down the side, and then along the bottom. By the time I had got halfway along the bottom I was feverish and it was all I could do to keep myself from grabbing up the chisel and prying the lock out. But I didn't want to do that. I wanted to take it out without damaging anything so I could put it back the way it was.

And then I was done. It had taken maybe two hours, but the wood covering the lock was gone. Now I picked up the screwdriver, slipped it gently under the lock, and pried very lightly. The lock raised up and slid out as easy as you please. Oh, it gave me a lovely feeling to have it work out so neat. I felt all tingly.

I set the lock down on Major Mattoon's desk next to the brass plate and the screws. I swung the cabinet door open, picked up the candle, and flashed it over the narrow drawers, looking at the labels. They said things like "Deeds," "Mass. Bonds," "Mortgages," "Notes and Loans," and so forth. I'd memorized the drawer the list was in. It was labeled "Miscellaneous." I pulled it open. The list was lying right there on top. Quickly I pulled it out, set the candle down on the desk, and looked at it, bending down to see it in the candlelight. Captain Shays' name came first. Peter's was fourth.

Now I snatched up a blank piece of paper from the pile on Major Mattoon's desk, took his pen out of his holder, and began copying. There were only eight names. Even as slow as I was at writing it didn't take me more than a couple of minutes to copy the names down. When I was finished, I waved the sheet of paper around to dry it, and then I folded it over and stuck it down the front of my shirt. I picked up the lock, pushed the cabinet door closed, and slipped the lock back into place. Quickly I put the brass plate back where it had come from and screwed it in place, making sure that I turned the screws down firmly so that the plate wouldn't accidentally come loose. Then I picked up the cloth and began wiping the spilled wax off the door. There was more of it than I had thought, and I had to scrape at it with my fingernails to get it clean. But in a few minutes everything was back to normal. I held the candle up to the cabinet and had a good look. You couldn't tell that it had been touched. I knelt down on the floor, unrolled the cloth, and began gathering the tools and the candle butts into it. And it was while I was doing that I heard a noise at the door and a voice said, "Justin."

Chapter Five

I SPRUNG TO MY FEET. IT WAS JASPER. HE was standing in the open door, leaning against the jamb and grinning. He was pretty drunk. The candle he was holding was tipped so that it was dripping wax on his pants, but he didn't notice. "Conkey," he said again. "Naughty boy. They hang naughty boys who break into the master's library and steal things."

"I'm not stealing anything," I said.

"Oh, no, not stealing anything. Just came in to read a book."

I couldn't think of anything to say.

He took a couple of steps away from the door to come after me, but he was swaying a lot from the liquor and he figured he'd better go back and lean against the doorjamb. "Conkey, you'll go to jail for this."

"I was looking for something that belongs to me," I said. I realized he didn't know I'd been working on the cabinet. He thought I'd been prowling around the desk.

"Oh, yes, Conkey. Major Mattoon's going to hear all of this in the morning."

"Major Mattoon won't be here in the morning," I said.

"You certainly know everything, don't you?"

"I know that," I said. "There's a thousand men gone down to Worcester to close the court there. They'll be there two or three days more at least. Major Mattoon won't come home until it's over."

He stared at me, blinking and swaying. "How do you know that?"

"I just know it," I said.

He didn't say anything. Then he said, "Where's my key?"

"In my pocket," I said.

"Give it to me." I took it out of my pocket and threw it to him. He tried to catch it, but missed completely. It bounced off his stomach and fell onto the floor. He started to bend down to pick it up, but he began to sway and had to straighten up again. "Pick that up and hand it to me proper," he said.

"No," I said. "You're not my master."

"You wait until I speak to Major Mattoon, Conkey. You'll wish you'd done what you were told. Now, pick it up."

"Jasper, why are you on Major Mattoon's side? Why aren't you on our side?"

He stared at me, trying to figure out what I was saying. "What were you looking for in here?"

"A paper," I said. "Major Mattoon tried to get Peter's oxen and now he's after his farm. He's got a mortgage on it. I was going to find the papers and burn them."

He grinned at me again. "Well, you got fooled. He keeps all his papers in that cabinet behind you. That's solid oak. You couldn't break into that with an ax."

"Why are you on his side?" I said. "Why aren't you on ours?"

"What are you talking about, Conkey?"

"You know what I'm talking about."

He stood there swaying and looking bleary, almost as if he was about to fall asleep. I didn't know if he had caught what I'd said. "The River Gods. They're trying to take our property. Me and Peter and Molly, and you, too."

He stared at me again, blinking. "Know why I'm on Mattoon's side?"

"Why," I said. I was surprised to hear him say, "Mattoon" without the Major.

"Because it's the only side I've got."

"I don't understand."

"You got a little property; Mattoon's got a lot. I don't have any at all. Who's going to take care of me if I lose this job? You and your sister and McColloch? You all going to take care of me? Feed me and clothe me?"

"We don't have anything extra."

"There you are," he said. "That's it. That's it right there." He put out one finger and waggled it at me. "Who's got extra? Why Mattoon, he's got extra."

"You could farm."

"Not without land. Can't farm without land, Conkey."

"You could go to work for somebody else."

He grinned. "Sure. Give up the fat life here and work in the fields fourteen hours a day for three shillings a day."

"At least you'd be your own man."

"Anybody who works in the fields fourteen hours a day isn't his own man, Conkey."

I didn't say anything.

He waggled his finger at me. Then he started to stagger, but grabbed hold of the doorjamb and straightened up. There was wax all over his breeches now. "No sir, Conkey. I'm with Mattoon. You fellows can go down to Worcester or Springfield or any other place and parade around if you want and maybe get shot by the militia, but not Jasper. I'm with Mattoon. He's the only side I got, Conkey."

I had to feel sorry for him, drunk as he was, and hard as he was on me. I guess I was about the only person he had to order around—me and the housemaid. "Well, all right," I said. "I understand. But the rest of us still have something to lose. We should stand up for our rights."

"Stand up for whatever you like, Conkey."

"You wouldn't try to stop us?"

"All I try is to mind my own business," he said. "You ought to try it, too."

"Are you going to tell Major Mattoon I was in here?"

He stared at me, blinking in the candlelight. "Where's my key?" he said slowly.

"It's on the floor." I stepped forward, picked it up, and handed it to him.

He held in in his hand and looked it over carefully. "You sure that's the right key?"

"Yes," I said. "Let's go out and we can try it in the lock." Quickly I knotted up the bundle with the tools and candle ends in it, came back to the door, took him by one arm, and helped him through it. As he went through the door he staggered against the jamb, but got himself straight again. I pulled the door shut. He turned around and tried to put the key in the keyhole, but he was too drunk. The key kept waving around in the air and didn't go anywhere near the hole. Finally I took his hand and guided it until the key went in. Then I helped him turn it.

He took the key out of the lock and fumbled it into his pocket. "No, Conkey, I won't tell Mattoon. You boys go ahead and parade around and get shot if you want. If that's what you want, I won't tell Mattoon." He turned away and staggered off down the hall, bumping the walls from side to side.

He didn't tell. For the next few days I was pretty careful to be cheerful and do what I was told. He never said anything. I wasn't sure why. Drunk as he was, he might have forgotten the whole thing. Or maybe he was afraid that if he told Major Mattoon I'd been in the library, I'd tell him that Jasper and the rest had been drinking up his wine. Or he'd have to explain how I got the key in the first place. But maybe he was partly on our side, too. I didn't know.

Anyway, I had another thing to worry about, which was that Major Mattoon knew that Peter was one of the leaders. Peter would be coming down to see me sooner or later. If he didn't have some reason for coming into Amherst, he'd make a special trip. And what would Major Mattoon say if he saw Peter on his property? Could he have him arrested, I wondered? It seemed to me pretty clear that I ought to get the list up to him as soon as possible. But how? I wasn't allowed to leave the place.

By the middle of the week there were all sorts of rumors around about what had happened at Worcester. It was said that the militia fired on our people, and that they didn't, that our people had burned the courthouse, and that they hadn't. Major Mattoon came home on Wednesday, but naturally he didn't say anything to us about it. And then on Saturday Peter came down. He just showed up at the kitchen as bold as could be, and asked for me. Jasper came and got me, frowning like mad at me and Peter, but he was afraid to say anything. I sneaked some bread out of the kitchen for Peter, and we went out into the woodshed and talked. As soon as we were safe in the shadows of the shed, I said, "I got it, Peter."

"What?"

"The list." I took it out and handed it to him. He opened it up and read it. "You're on it," I said.

"So I see. They're wrong about that. I'm just sort of an aide to Captain Shays."

"Well, they think you're one of the leaders. I was afraid for you to come down."

"They're not arresting anybody yet. They will be soon enough." He folded the paper up and put it in his shirt. "Good work, Justin," he said. It made me proud to have him say that.

Then he told me about Worcester. It seems that it went just about the same as Springfield. Our people had marched in and closed the court. There wasn't much the judges could do about it, so they had just gone away.

"We're winning then," I said.

Peter was gnawing at the bread. "Not really. We can't just go on closing the courts forever. Sooner or later they'll send an army out after us. What we've got to get are some real changes in the law. Something's got to be done about the taxes, something's got to be done about these debts everybody has and going to debtor's prison. *And* the court fees, *and* the legal fees, and all the rest of it. Somehow, the Governor and the General Court have got to get it through their heads that they can't go on treating us like this."

"What's going to happen, Peter?"

"Can't say. Don't know. But if we don't get some changes, I think there'll be war. The plain people won't stand for losing their oxen and cattle and their farms to the rich time after time. They'll fight. If a man loses his farm, what's he got left?"

"If there's fighting, I want to be in it."

He gave me a look. "No sir," he said. "You're too young."

"Peter, I'm not—"

"You've got your job to do here. You're more valuable here than fighting."

I decided not to argue about it. If it came to fighting, I was determined to go. "The way I fixed the lock to his cabinet I can always get into it again."

"That's fine. Don't take any chances. Wait until you get something good."

"Like what?"

"What we'd really like to know is what they plan to do—whether they're going to send an army out against us, whether they're going to use the militia on us, if they start planning to arrest people. Sooner or later they'll do something. That's what we want to know."

"All right," I said. "I'll try."

The next few weeks were a confusing time. All through September and into October there were meetings and speeches. Lots of the towns got up petitions which they sent to the Governor, asking redress for our grievances—

lower taxes, or lower court fees, and such. There were more court closings, too. Half the state of Massachusetts was in an uproar, with people arguing on all sides, everybody with his own opinion of what should be done. It was hard for us to know exactly what was going on, but we read about it in the *Hampshire Gazette,* and sometimes the men on the farm got gossip and rumors from the taverns or stores when they were out carrying shipments of flax or wheat or whatever to Springfield.

Then in October the Governor's Council put out a big proclamation that if any of the people who had been closing the courts would take an oath of loyalty before January 1st of the next year—1787—he would be pardoned for whatever he'd done to "make a disturbance." But anybody who wouldn't take the oath would be tried for high treason and if found guilty, suffer what the law called "condign punishment."

I asked Jasper what that meant. "'Condign' means 'suitable,' and the suitable punishment for treason is hanging."

"You mean they'd actually hang Pet—people?"

"That's what they're saying, Justin. I'd watch my step if I were you. Everybody knows that your brother-in-law is involved in the whole thing. They'll be keeping a sharp eye on you. You're both likely to get it in the neck."

I could feel the hair on the back of my neck sort of tingle—like it was standing straight out like the fur on a scared cat. I wondered if maybe things hadn't got out of hand. It was getting pretty clear that it had been a bad mistake for us not to send our representatives to the General Court.

But the proclamation didn't scare anybody. It just riled

all of our people up. And on October 13, Daniel Shays issued an order for organizing all of our people into a regular army. It said:

> Gentlemen,
>
> *By information from the General Court, they are*
> *determined to call all those who appeared to stop the Court*
> *to condign punishment. Therefore, I request you to assemble*
> *your men together, to see that they are well armed and*
> *equipped with sixty rounds each man, and to be ready to*
> *turn out at a moment's warning; likewise to be properly*
> *organized with officers . . .*

So the army was formed. All over our part of the state men began signing up, one company of a hundred or so men in this little town, another company in that one. Sometimes whole militia companies just went on drilling—but with the idea of fighting against the government instead of for it. Some of the men had good muskets leftover from when they'd fought in the Revolutionary War. Others had fowling pieces or flintlocks they used for hunting. Others didn't have anything but clubs or maybe a sword. But they were ready to fight.

Some people called our army the Shaysites, but most people called it the Regulators, because on the enlistment papers our soldiers were called "Regulators in Order for the Suppressing of Tyrannical Government of the Massachusetts State." The enlistment was supposedly for four months, with a pay of forty shillings a month and a bonus of forty pounds if we won. But nobody knew where the money to pay anybody was coming from, and anyway, a lot of men never bothered to sign the enlistment papers, but just went out and drilled with the rest. The really strange thing was the government was going to tax us to pay the militia. The Regulators would be paying their enemy to fight them.

I sure wanted to join up myself. It seemed like there was going to be a war for me to fight in after all. Maybe I'd really have a chance to do something brave that would make Peter proud of me. Of course, I wasn't old enough. But I knew of people who fought in the Revolution when they were only fourteen—drummer boys and such—and if they could do it, why not me?

And I was worrying about this, worrying about how I was going to get Peter to let me go, worrying about how I was going to escape from Major Mattoon's house, when one day there arrived three men on horseback. It was early November, about three o'clock in the afternoon. Major Mattoon greeted them at the front door, and then they all went back to the library and shut the door. I resolved that I was going to get in on the meeting.

Chapter Six

I WENT OUT TO THE PANTRY WHERE JASPER was sorting out napkins. "They probably want some wine, don't you think, Jasper?"

He gave me a look. "What are you up to, Justin? It isn't like you to beg for work."

"I just didn't want to get into trouble."

"If they want something, they'll ask for it."

"Well, I'd better bring up some wood."

"You mean there isn't any wood in the library?"

"Not very much," I said. "I forgot." That was a lie: there was plenty of wood in the library, for I was always taking more in, in hopes of spotting an important piece of paper on Major Mattoon's desk. "I'll get some."

"You'd better be quick about it."

I went out to the woodshed and in five minutes I was at the library door. I pushed it open with my foot and walked in. Major Mattoon and the three others were sitting at the table at the opposite side of the room from the desk. When I came through the door Major Mattoon gave me a look, but then went back to his conversation. I quietly set the logs down in the box that was there for them. Then I picked up the poker and began jabbing at the logs in the fireplace, as if to make them burn better.

"You fellows from Boston don't know how bad things have gotten out here," Major Mattoon said. "The whole countryside is on fire."

"Oh, I think Governor Bowdoin is well aware of your problems."

"We can't count on the militia. Half of them are in cahoots with Shays' Regulators. Hundreds of them drill with the militia, and then turn around the next day and drill with the Regulators."

I went on poking at the fire.

"We know that, Major Mattoon. We aren't counting on the militia, either."

"Then we're going to get our army, after all?"

"We thought you'd be pleased to hear that news."

"By God, sir, I am," Major Mattoon said. "That's the best news I've heard for months. We'll run the rabble back into their holes quick enough." Suddenly he noticed me. "Conkey, what are you doing?"

"Just fixing the fire, sir."

"That's enough, that's enough. Go along."

I put the poker back in its rack and walked toward the door, going softly in hopes of hearing just one more thing. I opened the door. "Oh, Conkey, tell Jasper to bring us in some port."

I went through the door. Then I raced out into the kitchen, downstairs to the wine cellar, and found a bottle of port. I took it up, wiped it off, then got the corkscrew and the tray and went back down the corridor toward the library. As I passed the pantry, Jasper looked up. "Where are you going with that?" he said.

"The Major asked me to bring them some port.".

"Are you sure he didn't say, ask Jasper to bring some in?"

"He asked me, Jasper." Jasper said nothing, and I walked back into the library. I opened the wine and began to fill the glasses.

"You have to think of them as children," I heard Major Mattoon say. "They run up debts buying gewgaws—fancy pins and silver buttons and similar trash coming in from abroad—and when they can't pay their taxes they complain about the laws."

I handed the glasses of port around.

"People with little or no property are not to be trusted. They don't know how to handle money," one of the men said.

I recorked the bottle. Then I slipped quietly over to the fireplace. There was a little hearth brush hanging there on a hook.

"They need to be kept under control," the Major said. "Or the first thing you know, they'll be out after our property. What we need is a well-disciplined army to keep order around here."

I began to sweep the bits of bark on the hearth into the fireplace, going as slow and quiet as I could.

"Well, we have one for you." I had my back to them, but I heard the rustle of paper. "Here's what Governor Bowdoin proposes to send you. General Benjamin Lincoln will have charge of the force. You know him, I assume?"

"Yes," Major Mattoon said. "He's an excellent choice."

I wanted to get a look at that paper. I knew it was about as important as anything could be. But I couldn't go on sweeping the hearth forever. I tried desperately to think of something else to do.

"The Governor is not holding back anything. He knows these people have to be taught a lesson. If every farmer who runs up debts is allowed to disown them with force of arms, there'll be no way to run a sound economy. The law has got to be enforced."

"You're right," another man said. "The common people must understand that the men who own the country are the men who should govern it. We must be firm here."

Oh, it made me angry to hear them talk like that, as if because we were just plain farmers we couldn't think things through for ourselves. Peter would have stood up and shouted at them, and I wanted to do the same. But then Major Mattoon said, "Conkey, stop fiddling with the broom and leave us."

"I was just cleaning up a bit, sir," I said.

"Just leave us." He turned to the other men. "It's just what I've been saying. You can't even trust your own servants anymore. The boy's brother-in-law is in the thick of it with the Regulators. Now obviously he's hanging about in hopes of picking up some scrap of information."

I blushed. "No sir, I was just—"

"I wasn't speaking to you, Conkey. You'll speak when spoken to. Now leave." I left, furious with them and raging inside. I was determined I'd get a look at that paper.

But how? With Major Mattoon already suspicious of me it wasn't going to be easy. I kept out of his way as much as possible the rest of the day. The three visitors stayed for dinner, and with that extra company, I had to help Jasper wait on table. There was a lot of talk about the Regulators and the chances of a real revolution, but most of it was just general talk and wasn't any help to me. After dinner the men went back to the library to drink their port, and I worked with Jasper cleaning up the dining room and washing the dishes. And all the while my mind was whirling: How was I going to get the library key? Because once I got into the library, I could have the lock out of the cabinet in two minutes. After that it would only take me five minutes to read over the paper with General Lincoln's plans on it, and another couple of minutes to put the lock back in the cabinet door. But how would I get into the library?

We put away the last of the dishes. "I'm going off," Jasper said. I figured he was going someplace with the maid. "Wash off the table and sweep up the dining room floor. Then you can go to bed." He left, and I got a wet rag, went into the dining room, and began washing the crumbs off the table top. A few minutes later, Major Mattoon and the three men came down the corridor and out toward the front door. The major gave me a look as they went through, but I just kept on working. I finished up the table and began sweeping the floor. I could hear Major Mattoon saying good-bye to his guests. Then in a moment he was coming back. "Conkey," he said, "clear the bottle and glasses out of the library when you finish here. I'm going to bed."

My heart began to quicken. "Yes, sir," I said. I took my time about sweeping up. I wanted to make sure Major Mattoon was really gone before I went into the library. When I heard his footsteps on the stairs, I got the dustpan out of the pantry, swept the crumbs into it, and dumped them into the fireplace. Then I went softly down the corridor to the library.

I stood in the middle of the room looking around. The dirty glasses and the empty port bottle stood on the table. The candles were burning low. For a moment I just listened. The house was silent. Major Mattoon had gone to bed. Still, I wanted to get it done as fast as possible. Quickly, I closed the library door, and then I went over to the desk. I needed something I could use for a screwdriver to get the screws out of the brass plate over the lock. There was nothing on the desk that would work. I knew that Major Mattoon would have a letter knife somewhere. I opened the top drawer to the desk. There was one there, among a jumble of pens and things. I took it out, and that was when the door slammed open and Major Mattoon and Jasper marched into the room. Jasper was carrying a pistol, and Major Mattoon was carrying a quirt.

"You cur, you little scum," the Major shouted. "I take you in to save McColloch's oxen and this is what you do to me. I should have known it all the time. I should have known from the start that you were spying on me."

I backed up against the cabinet. "I wasn't spying, sir." I was pretty scared.

"You little liar. Why did you think I told you to clear up in here?"

It had been a trap. I didn't say anything.

He came around the desk and put his face up close to mine. "Oh, I caught you that time, Conkey. And now I've got you. What have you taken of mine?"

"Nothing, sir. I haven't taken anything." I felt cold and dead white.

"Answer, what have you taken?" Jasper was standing

behind the Major, a bit at the side, holding the pistol. I wondered if he'd shoot if I tried to make a break for it.

All of a sudden Major Mattoon hit me across the face with the whip. My head jerked back and smacked against the cabinet. The whole side of my face stung like fury. "Answer me," he shouted.

"I never took anything," I said. I could feel blood trickling into my mouth.

"You liar. You dirty little liar. I'm going to beat you within an inch of your life." He raised the whip again. I ducked my head forward and covered my face with my arms. The whip cut across the top of my head. I tried to cover my head better. He swung again, the whip slashing across my arms and catching me on the forehead.

"Stop," I shouted. "Please stop."

"What have you stolen?"

"Nothing." I lowered my arms to look at him. There was blood on my shirt and when I touched my face, blood came away on my hands. One of my eyes ached horribly. I wondered if he had hurt it badly. "I never stole anything."

He stared at me. Then suddenly without warning he slapped upward with the whip and hit me under the chin. I filled with rage. "If you hit me again I'm going to kill you," I shouted.

He stared at me. "Shoot him, Jasper," he said. "I've caught him thieving in my house, I've a right to shoot him."

"Major—"

"Shoot him. He threatened to kill me."

"Major Mattoon, I—"

"That's an order, Jasper."

I looked at Jasper. He didn't raise the pistol. "I can't, Major."

"Then give me the pistol."

He turned to take the gun and I broke and ran. I bounced off the major, shoving him against the desk, and then I fled through the library door, through the darkened house, slamming into furniture, and out the front door into the yard. I ran on, down the long driveway under the line of trees, through the gate, and out onto the road. Then I stopped to look back. There was nobody behind me; nobody was following. I waited to see if I heard the sound of horses being harnessed, or people shouting. It was quiet. I began to jog up the road, heading for home.

Chapter Seven

 SO THAT WAS THE END OF THAT. I SETTLED back in at the farm. I was glad to be there, happy to be home, and happy not to have to take orders from Jasper and Major Mattoon. Of course, Peter was in a rage when he saw my face with the whip slashes on it. He wanted to go right into Amherst and beat Major Mattoon to a pulp. But Molly and I calmed him down, because we knew he might murder the major, or else get shot by somebody while he was doing it. The wounds would heal in time.

The next question was whether Major Mattoon would try to take the oxen again. Peter didn't think he would, at least not right away. "He won't try anything yet," he said. "He'll wait until we're beaten, and then he'll come after them. He won't forget, don't you worry."

And so we settled down to wait for the war we knew was coming. Neither side was giving in. The General Court passed a few laws which were supposed to help us, but they didn't really do very much. "Just a sop," Molly said. "Just throwing us a bone. They haven't given us anything." On our side, we went on closing the courts. Leastwise, Peter and the rest did. Peter still wouldn't let me get in on the fighting.

On November 21st a group of Regulators closed the court in Worcester. The next week they weren't so lucky. They tried to close the court at Concord, but at the last minute some of the Regulators backed out and the whole thing fell apart, and the court met and did its business. Worse, some of the leaders of that bunch of Regulators were caught by government troops and arrested. Peter got the story from Captain Shays and told it to us.

"They came out from Boston with a posse, maybe a hundred men, under Colonel Ben Hichborn and Colonel Henry Wood of the militia. They brought a sheriff with them, with writs for the arrest of some of the Regulator officers. They took them by surprise in a house they were staying at, and they captured Oliver Parker and Benjamin Page. But the most important of our fellows, Job Shattuck, got away. He cleared out of the house as the posse came in. It was getting to be night and freezing cold, and starting to snow. Shattuck went back down to Groton, where he lived, in the snowstrom and hid out in his own house.

The posse followed him down there. By the time they got there somebody had warned Shattuck that they were coming, and he cleared out of the house and made for a patch of woods that was nearby. When Colonel Wood saw that Shattuck was gone, he figured he might be in the woods, so he threw his troops all around it and began to close in. Well, Shattuck backed off and backed off until he came up against a creek that flowed through there. Cold as it was, there wasn't any use for him to swim it—he'd have frozen to death halfway across. Wood's men closed in. All

Shattuck had was an old broadsword. He drew it, and when the posse came up to him he didn't surrender, but began to fight. Wood's men would close on him and take a jab at him with their swords, and he'd slash back with his. It was ten against one, and when two or three of them came in on him at once, he was hard pressed to stave them off. He suffered a nick and then another more serious wound and finally one of Wood's men charged in and whacked him across the knee with his sword and cut through the knee cap and the ligaments, and down he went. They trussed him up and carried him off to jail in Boston and there he lies, and may be dead of his wounds already for all we know out here."

It was getting closer to a real war. On December 5th the court was to meet in Worcester again. Captain Shays— actually they were calling him General Shays now, because that was his rank in the Regulators—went down there with a force of men two or three days before the court was to meet. They stopped the court, but there was a raging blizzard that day, with sixteen inches of snow. It went on snowing for five more days—more snow than anybody had seen around here since the great snow of 1717, they said. And bitter cold, too. Lots of people who marched out with General Shays were frostbitten going home, and a man named William Hartley froze to death in the road in Northampton. The cold went on, and so did the court closings. On December 26th, General Shays went into Springfield once more with a small group of Regulators and closed the court there.

It kept looking more and more like a real war—another Revolution, only this time not against the British, but against our own Massachusetts government. There hadn't been any real battles yet, but the government had warrants out for the arrest of a lot of people, and government troops were going around trying to find them. They tracked some down and put them in jail. The sheriffs were still jailing people for debt, too. Right in Pelham the sheriff came and put a widow named Mrs. MacIntire out of her house and she had to go and live with the MacKenzies down the road. She was sick, too. You can guess how everybody felt about that. If they were going to put sick widows off their land, what would they do to the rest of us?

If there was going to be a war, I wanted to be in on it. I brought it up with Molly.

"Why can't I go?"

"Because Peter doesn't want you to, that's why. I don't want you to go, either. I've got enough to worry about that Peter might get hurt."

"What right has he got to order me around?" I said. "He's not my father."

"He's the head of the household and he can give any orders he wants."

"Why does that give him the right to order me around?" I said.

"Peter is responsible for our safety and well-being, and it's his job to see that things run right."

"Molly, you don't let him order you around."

She thought about that. "Mostly I do what he says; I only argue with him if he gets hasty and does something foolish."

"You mean you don't mind taking his orders?"

"He's my husband. I'm supposed to be a help to him."

"But you don't *have* to," I said.

"You don't understand, Just—I want to. You seem to

forget that Peter is a good man. Everybody around Pelham admires him. He's just hasty with his feelings. Sometimes he acts too quick. But he's a better man than most. So don't take it so hard if he tells you what to do. He thinks that so long as he's the father here it's his job to make things run right. Whoever is in charge has to be able to give orders so that everybody does his proper share of the work and gets his proper share of things out of it."

I thought of something. "Well, what about Governor Bowdoin, and Major Mattoon and the General Court? Do you think it's right to tax away people's oxen and flax that they grew and even their farms, just because they're in charge?"

"What do *you* think," she said. "You know how I feel about the government."

"But they're in charge. If Peter has a right to give orders because he's in charge, why don't they have the right, too?"

"Because," she said. "Because if you're in charge you're supposed to use your power for the good of everybody, not for the good of yourself. That's the difference. The difference between Peter and Major Mattoon. Peter gives you orders, but he's on your side, and trying to see that things go right for you. Major Mattoon gives orders just to get the best for himself. That's wrong. The one who's in charge ought to be looking out for everybody."

We were quiet for a minute. Then I said, "I still want to go."

She looked at me. "Want to be a hero, do you?"

I blushed. "I want to do my share," I said.

She sat silent. "Well," she said finally. "I'll think about it."

So we waited—waited to see if General Lincoln was

really coming out with an army. January and the new year, 1787, came. And then we heard that the army was coming.

We talked about it over supper one night. The two little ones were sitting on a bench in front of the fireplace, staying warm and eating dried apples. We had pulled the table up close to the fire, too. The wind was driving the cold through the cracks around the windows, and outside the branches of the trees were thrashing about in the moonlight, which was bright on the snow. "They will be coming after us now," Peter said. "They mean to put us down once and for all. They could get thousands of men from Boston out against us."

"Thousands?" I said.

"According to the order, the Governor was to raise forty-four hundred troops, but we don't know exactly how many he can actually get," Peter said. "You can be sure that they won't come out here with less than they think are needed to do the job."

"What is Daniel Shays planning?" Molly said.

Peter shrugged. "My guess is that he'll take us to Springfield again. General Sheppard has called up the militia there and has taken over the Congress arsenal. He wouldn't have done that on his own. Governor Bowdoin must have ordered it. Of course, they didn't want us to get hold of the arms stored there. My guess is that Shays will try to take the arsenal. It's the logical thing to do. There are cannons stored there and with cannons and plenty of powder and shot we might stand a chance against Sheppard."

"There'll be fighting," Molly said. "There'll be killing."

Peter looked at her and then away. "Maybe," he said. "Maybe not. I know that Daniel Shays hasn't much heart for fighting. He'll do nearly anything to avoid a pitched battle. I think what he's really hoping is that the militia will come over to us. If they did that, and we took the arsenal, chances are that anyone they send out from Boston would be willing to negotiate, and we might get what we want without fighting."

"That's a lot of maybe's," Molly said. "When you have a lot of men standing around with muskets in their hands, sooner or later there's going to be shooting."

"Not necessarily," Peter said.

"You'll have to go, won't you, Peter," she said.

"Of course," he said, shoveling in a mouthful of corn-meal mush. "Everybody's got to do their share. I couldn't sit home and let the other fellows do my fighting for me." He swallowed. "Besides, General Shays is counting on me. I've got a good horse, and he knows I don't mind fighting."

I stared down at my plate, trying to think how to say it. I was scared of the idea of getting shot at, and scared of going against Peter anyway, but when else was I going to have a chance to do something brave? "I'm going, too," I said.

Nobody said anything. Then Peter said, "No, you're not."

"Peter, I've got a right to—"

He bashed his hand down on the table. "I said you're not going."

"Peter—"

Molly touched my arm. "Hush up, Just," she said. She laid down her spoon. "Why can't he go, Peter?"

"Because I'd never forgive myself if I let him get killed."

"What's the difference between my getting killed and your getting killed, Peter?" I said.

"Men have to take their chances. Not boys."

"Peter," Molly said, "he's almost a man."

"Not yet he isn't."

"All right," Molly said. "He can stay here and look after the little ones. I'll go."

Peter's jaw began to jut out. "The hell you're going," he said. "I'm not having my wife parading about like a man."

"Why not? Why shouldn't I go? I know how to shoot a musket."

"I don't care if you know how to shoot a cannon. You're not going."

"Yes, I am," she said. "I'm going to put on men's clothing and go. You can't stop me. You won't know it's me."

He was getting in a rage and I knew that in a minute he was going to hit her. "Peter, calm down," I said.

He didn't even hear me. "Just drop the subject, Molly," he said.

"I won't," she said. "I'm going. I'm going to dress up in—"

He reached across the table and smacked her across the face with the palm of his hand. It made a loud crack. I'd never seen him hit her before. We all sat deathly still, Peter and Molly staring at each other and me looking down at my plate. One of the little ones looked at Molly and began to whimper.

Peter stood up. "I'm sorry," he said. "But the two of you would make a man insane."

Molly went on staring at him. "If I don't go, will you let him go then?"

He threw his arms up as if he were flinging an armful of leaves in the air. "All right, all right, if he wants to see what war is like, let him. Once he gets shot at the first time there won't be so much talk about standing up for his rights." He stalked out of the room.

The next day I went down to Uncle Billy's tavern and signed up. After that, I went over regularly with Peter to drill. Of course, I didn't have a musket, but I had my father's sword, and I took that. There wasn't much glory in drilling—it was all marching and countermarching back and forth in the snow, with a bitter wind blowing about half the time. It was a hard winter, one of the worst for years. It's a funny thing, but when you imagine war, you always think about it's being in the summer. It's hard to take an interest in it when your fingers and toes are about to freeze off.

In the middle of January, companies of Regulators under their own officers began to gather in Pelham. They slept around in barns and at people's houses wherever there was room. The whole town was on Shays' side. When the weather wasn't too bad, they drilled on the open field in front of Uncle Billy's tavern.

Peter and I spent our free time trying to get things in order for Molly, especially making sure that there was enough wood up. We cut the wood into four-foot logs and put them into stacks four feet high and eight feet long. That's one cord of fuel wood, and that little farmhouse would use twenty-five cords in a normal winter for cooking and heating. It was an awful lot of chopping and sawing. "I figure it'll all be over one way or another in a couple of days," Peter said. "But you never can tell. We might not go at all. Shays is waiting until the last minute before he does anything."

"How long will he wait?"

"He can't wait much longer. The Governor has ordered out General Lincoln, and he's already marching for

Springfield. If we're going to take the army we'll have to do it before he arrives. General Sheppard's only got a thousand or so militia at the arsenal now, but if he has Lincoln with him, too, we won't stand a chance."

It worried me that we might not go at all. It seemed like it could all get called off. But finally General Shays gave the order, and on Monday, January 22, we marched out of Pelham. Our war against the government had begun.

I wasn't the only one without a musket. Some of the men had only swords, too, and some just clubs. Many of those with muskets didn't have bayonets. As Peter said, it was the bayonets that counted. You'd fire off two or three volleys, but it was the bayonet charge afterward that got you the victory. And what kind of a charge could we make without bayonets? It scared me pretty good when I thought about it.

The weather was still bad. There was three feet of snow on the fields and the roads were deep in frozen mud. It was like marching on heaps of jagged stones—your feet kept twisting and turning under you. The sky was cloudy and we knew it was going to snow before the day was over.

How long it would take us to get to Springfield I didn't know. Nobody was sure exactly what General Shays was planning. The men marching beside me had a lot of different ideas. It seemed that we were to march to Wilbraham, which was twenty-five miles from Pelham on the road from Boston. That way we could get between Lincoln's army and Sheppard's men at the arsenal. Other Regulators would march down the Connecticut River, and some others were on the other side at West Springfield. That way we would have the town nearly surrounded.

From Wilbraham, our group would march to

Springfield. Of course, there was an awful lot of guessing about what would happen when we got there—whether the militia would fire on us or join us, or what. "They won't fire on us," one man said. "Shays is counting on that. You can bet he won't fight unless he has to. He'll try to parlay with them as long as he can."

We marched on through Belchertown and Palmer and into Wilbraham. Here we found other men. It kept getting colder and colder. Our feet and fingers were numb, and the men were holding their hands over their faces to prevent their cheeks and noses from getting frostbitten.

There were some towns around the western part of the state that weren't with us—places where the people were against the Regulators and supported the government. But most places were with us. Wilbraham was one. We got there in the late afternoon, and the people there put us up in their houses and barns and fed us the best they could with corn bread and smoked meat and whatever else they could spare. Our company was quartered in a barn. It wasn't bad. The cattle helped to keep it warm, and if you snuggled down in the hay you could be pretty comfortable.

Sometime after dusk Peter came around looking for me. He put his head in the door. "Are you in there, Justin?"

I could see it was him from the moonlight, and I went to the door. "Well," he said, "how do you like war so far?"

"I'd like it better in the summertime," I said.

"Oh, the weather is going to get a lot worse than this," he said. "This is nothing. It's supposed to snow tomorrow."

"Where are you quartered?"

He grinned. "I'm in a nice warm house. I'm attached to General Shays as an aide-de-camp."

"That's pretty lucky," I said.

"It's because of Brother. He wants a man with a good horse nearby for messages."

"Has General Shays said what we're going to do in Springfield?"

"I don't think he knows any more than anybody else. We'll probably march into Springfield on Wednesday. We expect to link up with Luke Day's people."

"Will we fight?"

"Don't know. General Shays will try to negotiate if he can."

"I wish I had a gun," I said.

"You should have thought of that back in Pelham," he said. "I'm going to get some sleep. See you in the morning."

We spent Tuesday in Wilbraham. It snowed in the morning and then it turned to rain in the afternoon. There wasn't anything to do but sit around the barn. Some of the men in my company had fought in the Revolution and we sat around listening to them tell stories about it.

We spent Tuesday night in the barn again and then around noon on Wednesday we formed up and began to march toward Springfield. It was cloudy and cold and likely to snow again. The snow in the field had a hard crust on it. The crust was sharp as a knife. It could cut you if you weren't careful.

But I wasn't thinking about the snow, I was thinking about Springfield. In a few hours we would be there. Would we fight? Would I have to go hand-to-hand with my sword against a militiaman with a bayonet? What would it feel like to have a bayonet go through you? Would I run if someone came after me? I didn't feel much like a hero: my mouth was dry and my innards cold as ice.

Chapter Eight

 ABOUT FIFTEEN MINUTES AFTER WE GOT started, just as we were moving out of Wilbraham, the line came to a halt. There were horsemen at the front of the column, and the legs of the horses were getting scraped and cut by the frozen slush. An order came back for our company to send forward some men to break down the crust in front of the horses. I was picked, and went up to the front.

There was a line of horse tracks and a trail of blood in them going down the road ahead of us, where somebody riding fast had passed along there. The blood had come from the horse's legs where they had gotten scraped by the snow crust. We figured it was a messenger riding to General Sheppard to tell him we were coming. We linked arms to be as close together as possible and walked forward, tromping down the snow crust. I liked being in front of the whole army. It made me feel sort of proud. But I knew it would make me a pretty easy target if I were still up there at Springfield.

It was slow going. We were setting the pace, and we couldn't make much time tromping down the snow. Springfield was right on the Connecticut River. We were still in the hills above the river. When the wind blew through the hills it froze our faces. We walked on, and after about three hours we began to see smoke from the buildings in Springfield in the distance. I wondered which one was the arsenal. Then the road dipped downward and we lost sight of the river and the town. We marched on. Finally, we came to a long slope and the buildings came closer alongside the road. As we came along past the few farms on the outskirts of the town, there were people standing in doorways and peering out of windows to watch us. I wondered whose side they were on.

We marched forward. We were on the Boston Road, which ran right into town. It was the biggest place I'd ever been to. There were lots of shops along the street we were marching on—an apothecary shop with jars of medicines in the window, a cooper who made barrels, and lots of taverns. We passed a big dry-goods store with a huge window in the front. I could see shelves of books and pewter mugs and dishes and bolts of cloth. Each store had its own colorful sign with some kind of a picture on it to tell you what kind of a store it was—a barrel for the cooper, a mortar and pestle for the apothecary, and so forth. It all seemed so pleasant. I wished I could stop in the stores and look around. I resolved that if we ended up not fighting I would take the time to visit the shops.

Here, too, the people stood in doors and windows and watched us. They didn't say anything, but just watched us march by. I wondered what they were thinking. I wondered if they hated us, or were afraid of us, or were glad that we were going to fight the militia.

Now the Boston Road began to rise. Somewhere up there was the arsenal. There was a cry of "Halt," and the line stopped. We looked ahead. The road curved so that we couldn't see very far. As we watched, a horseman in military uniform appeared around the bend and stopped. I turned around to look back. General Shays, wearing his buff and blue uniform from the Revolution, was sitting on his white horse talking to some of his officers. Then he began to move forward. Those of us who had been up front breaking the snow crust stepped aside to let him through. He was coming right by me, and as he got to me he noticed me. "Justin," he shouted, "Run along before my horse and stomp down that crust." Actually, there wasn't much snow crust here. Once we'd got in the town it had been pretty trampled already.

I felt a thrill that he'd picked me, and proud that I was out there, just me and General Shays. I stomped along at high speed, tromping down the snow even though there wasn't much need of it. Within a minute I was sweating and breathing hard, but I hardly noticed. Finally, I came up to the horseman and stepped aside.

General Shays stopped his horse. "How are you, Buffington?" he said to the horseman. He was also wearing a Revolutionary War uniform. It seemed funny to have two enemies dressed the same. I figured that he and General Shays had known each other in the Revolution.

Buffington looked at General Shays. "You see I am here

in defense of that country you are endeavoring to destroy."

General Shays stared back. "If you are in defense of the country, we are both defending the same cause."

"I expect we shall take different parts before evening," Buffington said.

"The part I take will be the hill on which the arsenal stands."

"You will meet a very warm reception," Buffington said.

"Will you fire?" General Shays said.

"Yes, undoubtedly."

"That's all I want to know," General Shays said. He wheeled his horse around, heading back to the column, and I ran back behind him through the crushed snow. My mind was all whirling. Buffington had said they would fire. Within a few minutes people would be shooting at me.

Now we snow-crushers were ordered into our regular ranks. We dashed back and the line started to move forward again. The men around me were envious that I had had a chance to find out what was going on, and they kept asking me questions out of the sides of their mouths. We weren't supposed to talk in ranks.

"Buffington said they would fire on us," I said.

"I don't believe it," one man said.

"Bluffington" another said. "Sheppard won't dare order the militia to fire. Most of them will come right over to us if he does."

"Quiet in the ranks," an officer shouted. We marched on. In a moment we came around the curve, and there ahead of us, on the top of the hill, was the arsenal. All along

I had thought that the arsenal was one building, but actually it was several buildings. In front of them was a wooden palisade which looked to be new: I figured they'd put it up especially to defend the arsenal against us. And in front of the palisade was a line of militiamen. In the midst of the militia were some cannons. The cannons seemed to be staring straight down the hill at me, as if I was their main enemy.

The column stopped. Two horsemen rode down the slope toward us, and two of our officers, also on horseback, went out to meet them. The four men stood together in the road for a minute, talking and gesturing. Then the meeting broke up and our men came back to us. We started marching again, moving step by step toward the arsenal. I couldn't take my eyes off those cannons. We kept on marching. Were we going to march right into the line of militia? Would they fire?

Then there was a great booming noise and a puff of smoke that rolled out of the blank eye of one of the cannons. The line sort of shuddered. Some men jumped to the side of the road or went flat. Quickly we realized that the cannon shot had been aimed above us. The men jeered and started marching again. In a moment there was another boom and another puff of smoke at the mouth of a cannon. But again the shot was aimed over us. "See, they won't fire on us," a man near me said.

Then came a third boom and another puff of smoke, and after it a long shriek and some shouts and cries. The line stopped. Ahead there was confusion in the ranks. Some men had flung themselves flat, some had jumped to the side of the road, some had crouched down, their weapons at the ready, prepared to receive a charge. I didn't know what to do, but I knew they were firing on us, and would probably fire again. I knelt down. Some of our men began to run toward me, going back down the hill. I looked forward. Now there were no men standing, and I could see all the way up. There was a body in the road. He was shuddering and jerking his arms and legs back and forth.

Then there was another boom and this time a long, eerie shriek, which seemed to go on and on, and I knew that another man was dying. I fell flat, my hands over my head. All around me there was the sound of running feet. I raised up my head. Our troops were pouring back down the hill away from the arsenal. I heard a voice shout, "Boys, stand fast. We can gain the day yet. Stand fast." There was the sound of a horse's hooves. It was General Shays. I leaped to my feet and the next thing I knew I was running, too, a part of the mob fleeing back down the hill. General Shays had reined up his horse and was waving his sword over his head. "Stand fast, boys," he shouted. Nobody paid him any attention. We just ran down the hill and began to spread out through the streets of Springfield like a stream of water breaking into rivulets on a slope.

I stopped, my breath coming hard in my lungs, and looked around. There was no more cannon fire and the militia didn't seem to be chasing us. Back up the hill, General Shays and a couple of officers were still wheeling about on their horses, trying to reorganize the few men still remaining. A few were forming up again around them, maybe fifteen or twenty. I stood watching, feeling scared and ashamed of myself, about as ashamed as I'd ever been. I'd had my chance to be a hero and instead I'd run. I couldn't have fought: nobody was about to fight. But I could have stayed at the top of the hill and tried to keep the others from running. Even if I'd just knelt in the road and stayed there, it would have been a sign that I was brave. But I'd run like the rest, just turned tail like a coward. I wondered if General Shays had noticed me.

I stood there in the road trying to decide what to do. Up ahead, General Shays had got his little group of men together. They were crouched in the road, their muskets at the ready. I was too far down the hill now to see the arsenal. I wondered if the militia were going to fire on them. One cannon shot could wipe them all out. All of a sudden I couldn't stand being a coward anymore. I didn't care if I got killed. I started forward up the road, feeling scared to death. I hunched down as low as I could. But I had only gone a few paces when the little group up the road rose and began to jog down the road toward me. General Shays and the other horsemen were coming along with them. They had given up. I had missed my chance.

Then I noticed that one of the horsemen was Peter. That made me feel even worse. I didn't want him to see me. I jumped off the road and ran around behind a small house. Crouching, I could see the men go by, looking grim. Peter's jaw was jutted forward, his face was smeared with mud and melting snow, and there was a long tear in his trousers. Then they were gone. I came out of hiding and went down after them. The question was where to go next. The militia might come after us at any minute. Then, too, General Lincoln's troops would be along, probably in a few hours. There was no telling how close they were. The day was about over now and it was getting dark. It was cold and great heavy clouds drooped low over us. It was going to snow. I would have to find some shelter or risk freezing to death. Where was I to go? I began to walk the rest of the way down the hill.

There were still a good many of our men milling around. Some were standing in little groups talking, some had hidden behind houses and were coming out. I stopped at one little cluster. One man was saying, "The word is around that Shays is going to make a stand in Pelham. We're supposed to go north up the river road toward Hadley and cut over from there."

"How do you know that?" somebody asked. I noticed he wasn't much older than me.

"Somebody I know got it from Shays. We're supposed to clear out of Springfield before Lincoln shows up with his troops."

"That much makes sense, anyway," the young fellow said. Everybody sort of nodded and in a minute we started walking through the streets of Springfield toward the river road. I knew we were in for a tough time. There would be snow and cold and we'd have difficulty finding a place to sleep.

The young fellow had noticed me join the group and he dropped back to walk beside me. "You're pretty young to be fighting," he said.

"I'm not much younger than you are," I said.

"I'm sixteen," he said.

"Well, I'm fifteen," I lied.

"You don't look it," he said. "Were you on the hill?"

"Yes," I said.

"I guess you ran, too."

I didn't like to answer that, but I had to. "Yes," I said. "Did you?"

"I wasn't going to stay up there if nobody else was."

"Neither was I," I said. To get off that subject I asked him where he was from, and we got to talking. His name was Levi Bullock and he was from Lanesboro, a village in the northwestern corner of the state. In that area most nearly everybody was on our side. We talked about that and walked along. There were little groups of men everywhere, some jogging along in a rush, others walking slowly. Most of them were heading for the river road to go north. Soon we reached the river and turned north. People kept joining our group and by the time we cleared Springfield there were fifty of us. By now it was dark and the cold was biting.

"We can't walk all night," somebody said. "We ought to start looking for a barn."

"I'd rather get well clear of Lincoln's men before we stop," Levi said. He reached into his coat pocket and took out a pipe and pouch of tobacco. "I wouldn't want to get caught in a barn by them. They might decide to burn us out." He stuffed some tobacco into his pipe with his thumb, and lit it with a couple of sparks from a flint. He looked pretty grand smoking the pipe. I envied him. I resolved I would try it the first chance I got.

"Lincoln will probably spend the night in Springfield. He won't march out tonight. We'd be safe in a barn."

But most people figured we'd better keep going, and we did. I was pretty tired. We'd marched all day and got shot at by cannons, and now we were walking again. I'd been on my feet for twelve hours. And I was hungry, too. I hadn't had anything much to eat all day—a few bits of bread, some dried apples, and a little bit of meat I'd brought from home. I wondered what would happen if we went to a farmhouse and begged for something to eat. The trouble was that we didn't know if the people around there were on our side or not.

We went through a couple of villages and then we came to South Hadley. The houses began to draw together. "There's a nice tavern up ahead," somebody said. "Might be able to get a mug of rum to warm us up."

"Doubt it," another said. "That's Noah Goodman's. He's a government man. He's not likely to do anything for us."

Nobody said anything further. We walked on. As we came into the village itself I noticed that some of the houses were shuttered up tight. I guessed that the people who lived in them were afraid of us—afraid of all the stragglers coming through their village. Men must have been coming along the road for a half an hour already, and they'd be coming the rest of the night. "They've shut up their houses," I said.

"They're worried," Levi said. "They don't know what to expect from us."

"I thought most of these towns were with us."

"Most of them are, but there's still a lot of people who are against us."

Just at that moment there was the sound of a gunshot somewhere up ahead of us. We ducked off to the side of the road and crouched low. There was no further sound.

"We ought to send a couple of scouts on ahead to reconnoiter," somebody said. It was sort of funny being in an army without leaders, where everything had to be talked over before we could do anything.

"Who wants to go?"

I was scared. It could be a party of Lincoln's men up there. But I was tired of being a coward. I started to say something, but it came out a rough squeak.

"I'll go," Levi Bullock said.

I cleared my throat.

"I'll go, too," came another voice in the dark.

"That'll be enough, then. The rest of us will cover the road. If we don't hear anything of you in fifteen minutes, we'll come up."

Levi trotted off into the darkness. I'd missed my chance again. Why had I let myself stand there thinking about it instead of just blurting out that I'd go, the way Levi had? Why hadn't I just burst out with it? Would I never get over being a coward? Would I be a coward all my life? The other men crouched down by the side of the road, and I crouched down with them, feeling miserable.

We waited. We heard another gunshot, but that was all—no shouting or shrieking. In about two minutes we heard somebody running toward us. It was Levi. "There's a couple of government men up there in Goodman's tavern. They're shooting at anybody they see along the road."

"All right," somebody said. "Let's split into two groups. About half of you swing off the road and circle around back. The rest of us will go straight up the road and give them a couple of balls through the windows. When you fellows around back hear the shots, break in from the rear and take the place. There'll be rum in there and a hot fire, and maybe some food as well."

That sounded cheerful enough. I decided that the bravest thing was to go with the men around back, because we might have to fight the men inside hand to hand. I lifted my sword in the scabbard to make sure it wasn't stuck. We cut off the road through the snow, which wasn't much fun, cold and deep as it was, and the crust likely to cut you to the bone. We got well out into the middle of the field which ran along the road and turned parallel to the road. Dark as the sky was, it was difficult to see very much at all, but a couple of times we saw spots of light near the road and knew we were passing along behind houses. Then we saw a large patch of light.

"That must be the tavern." We turned back across the field. We had to go through a small orchard, so our faces were continually being slapped by branches. When we came out of the orchard we could make out the shape of the tavern. There were four windows along the back and a blank space in the middle which we figured to be the door. We waited. Then came the gunshots—first one, then another, then a third. We couldn't tell whether it was our men or not. Suddenly the rear door of the tavern burst open. Two men dashed out and disappeared in the darkness. We charged forward and into the tavern. I had my sword out. I was the third one through the door. I raised my sword over my head, but the tavern was empty.

Chapter Nine

WE SPENT THE NIGHT IN THE TAVERN. IT was risky: Nobody knew where Lincoln's troops were, nobody knew if the people who owned the tavern would gather together their friends and try to drive us out. We took turns standing guard—one by the back door to watch the fields, one out front on the road. But still, dark as it was, a company of men could easily creep in close and take us by surprise.

But in spite of the risk, we stayed. We were cold and tired and wet and hungry, and the tavern was warm and the fire bright. There was food in the pantry and rum in the barrels. We roasted a pig over the fire and ate hunks of the meat with bread dipped in the grease. I drank some rum and hot water, too. I'd never drunk rum before, only cider. It made me sort of dizzy. I lay down in front of the fire and went to sleep.

Nobody bothered us all night. In the morning we got up and ate what was left of the pig and some dried fish we found. Then we took all the rest of the food we could find and divided it up so each man could have a share. I got some cheese, dried fish, and bread, which I wrapped up in a napkin from the tavern cupboard. Taking food was stealing, but Levi Bullock said, "They fired on us. Taking food from the enemy isn't stealing."

Outside, the winter clouds were low and dark. Nobody wanted to leave the fire, but we couldn't stay any longer. Sooner or later Lincoln would come after us. So we left and walked on toward Pelham. In about a half an hour it began to rain. In five minutes I was soaked through. The rain went on, and then it turned to sleet, which stung my face and hands when it hit. We walked out of South Hadley. It rained and sleeted all the while. I was soaking wet and I knew that if it turned a little bit colder my clothes would freeze to my body. Finally we got to the village of Hadley itself. We didn't know whether the people there would be for us or against us. There was a tavern there and a row of houses and a couple of stores. Two of the men went into the tavern and after a couple of minutes one of them came to the door and waved us in. He was grinning. "They're with the Regulators around here," he said.

We went in and dried ourselves off as best we could, taking turns by the fire. The tavern keeper gave us rum and hot water to warm us up, and we felt a lot better when we left. We kept up a good, brisk marching pace, so as to keep warm and get to Pelham as soon as possible. We made it in four hours. The Regulators had set up headquarters in Uncle Billy's tavern. Peter was there. When I walked in with the others he shouted, "Justin." He threw his arms around me and lifted me off the ground. I was surprised. I had figured he'd hate me for running off while he'd been brave and stayed. But he was just glad that I was alive and well.

"I'm sorry I ran," I said.

He put his hand on my shoulder. "You weren't the only one."

"That doesn't matter. I'm sorry I did it."

"Don't worry about it," he said.

I didn't say anything for a little bit. Then I said, "Did you tell Molly?"

"No," he said. "I just told her I hadn't seen you. She's pretty worried about you."

"But you saw me run."

"I wasn't noticing very much. I was pretty busy."

He was just saying that, I could tell. He'd seen me break and run.

"So, Justin. Had enough of war?"

I looked at him, surprised. "Oh, no," I said. "No, no, Peter, I want to stay." I just couldn't quit until I'd made up for being a coward.

He gave me a long look. "After all this you want to stay?"

"Oh, yes," I said.

"It's likely to be pretty bad from here on out. That business at the arsenal wasn't anything. We're likely to see some real fighting. You haven't even got a musket."

"I have father's sword. Lots of men don't have muskets."

"That won't be much help when they're shooting at you."

"Peter, I want to stay."

He thought about it. Then he said, "All right."

After that he took us over to a barn where we were going to be quartered. Uncle Billy Conkey's tavern was on

East Hill. The barn was next to the church on West Hill, just across a little valley from the tavern. General Shays was putting troops on both hills so he could fire down on people coming up the valley.

There were some other men in the barn when we got there. One of them was another fellow about the same age as Levi and me. He was from Porterfield, a place near Levi's hometown. Levi knew him. His name was Tom Mayo. Levi introduced us. We shook hands. I wondered if he'd run, but it wasn't right to ask.

We slept together in the barn that night and in the morning they sent me and Levi and Tom over to the tavern to pick up our breakfast rations. We brought the rations back to the barn. After we had eaten I said, "There's a cemetery behind the church. My great-great-grandfather is buried in that cemetery. Do you fellows want to see his grave?"

We went out to the cemetery. It was deep in snow, but the crust was thick and hard and you could walk on it if you stepped carefully. My great-great-grandfather's headstone was covered with snow almost to the top. I kicked through the crust and pushed the snow away from the stone with my hand. We could read the engraving:

> IN MEMORY OF ALEXANDER CONKEY
> DIED DEC. 3, A.D. 1758
> AGED 81 YEARS

"When my father was a little boy he used to take him for rides on his horse," I said. "He was born in 1677. There wasn't anything but Indians out here then. The country was practically new then."

"Imagine being buried in a town that didn't even exist when you were born," Levi said.

"If I get killed in the fighting, I'll be buried here," I said. "There's a lot of Conkeys in this graveyard."

"You figure you might get killed?" Tom Mayo said.

"We all might get killed," Levi said.

But I knew it was especially me who was likely to be killed. If you want to be a hero, you have to take chances.

That was Saturday. We did a little drilling, but mostly we sat around, rested up, and put our weapons in order. I borrowed a whetstone from the tavern and spent some time sharpening my sword, even though it didn't need it, just to have something to do. Sunday was the same—weather cold and clear but windy, so nobody wanted to spend much time outdoors. Levi and Tom and I took care of getting the rations. We didn't mind, because it gave us a chance to find out what was going on. General Shays had made Peter an officer, probably because he hadn't run from the arsenal fighting, so he usually knew what was happening.

When we came for rations Monday night, Peter told us that peace might be coming. General Rufus Putnam, Daniel Shays' old commander during the Revolution, had come over that afternoon under a flag of truce. Putnam and Shays had discussed peace terms. "Putnam wants us all to lay down our arms," Peter told us. "General Shays is all for it. He hasn't got any stomach for fighting Lincoln's troops. He told Putnam we'd give up and take an oath of allegiance to the government if the government will give all of us an unconditional pardon, and the militia is disbanded until the General Court can act on our grievances. Now we'll see what Lincoln has to say about it."

But Lincoln said no. Tuesday morning, Peter came

around to our barn and made the announcement. He stood in the door with the bright sunlight gleaming off the snow behind him, and the men sat in the hay and listened.

"You fellows have probably heard that General Shays tried to make a bargain with Lincoln so's we could avoid a fight. He said we'd be willing to take the oath of allegiance if they'd give us all an unconditional pardon and send Lincoln's army home until the General Court can act on our grievances." He took a deep breath. "I'm sorry to say that Lincoln has turned the proposal down. I'm supposed to tell you all that anybody who takes an oath of allegiance before a justice of the peace within the next three days will get a pardon. That's the only deal Lincoln is willing to offer us—if we surrender he won't hang us." He turned and spit out into the snow. "Now, I don't know what you fellows think about that kind of a bargain, but General Shays isn't going to quit and I'm not going to quit and most of the other men I've talked to aren't going to quit."

He stared around at us as we sat in the hay. I couldn't see his face very well because of the brightness of the light behind him, but I was pretty sure his jaw was jutting out. "Of course, I wouldn't want to influence any of you. It's up to each man to decide for himself." He turned and walked away.

Tom and Levi and I talked about it after Peter left. "I wonder why Lincoln wouldn't agree to Shays' plan? Tom said. "What's he got to lose by just waiting until the General Court has a chance to take up our grievances?"

"That's obvious," I said. "Lincoln figures he can beat us now, and maybe he won't be able to beat us later."

"You think we're going to get beat?" Tom said.

"I didn't say *I* thought so. I said that's what Lincoln probably figures."

Tom shook his head. "It still doesn't make sense. I mean, why fight if you don't have to?"

"Well, I don't know," I said. "Maybe he figures we won't fight. Maybe he figures we'll just give up."

"No, that's not it," Levi said. He'd got out his pipe and was tamping tobacco into it, being careful not to spill any in the hay where he'd lose it. "What it is is that people who have power and money don't like people without it to be rebellious. They like poor people to do what they're told without making a fuss."

"I don't believe that's so," I said. "I mean, the government's supposed to represent us. It's not like when we were under King George and the British. We're not supposed to do what the General Court wants us to do— they're supposed to do what we want *them* to do. The government is supposed to see that everybody gets a fair shake."

"Why?" said Tom.

"Because," I said. "That's the way it's supposed to be. We elect them to put in the laws we want to have, and if they don't pass the laws we want, why we can diselect them."

Levi got out his flint and struck it, and after a bit he got his pipe going and puffed out some smoke. I envied him smoking. I was tempted to ask for a puff, but I decided I'd better practice on my own before I tried in front of anybody. "Supposed to be is just supposed to be," he said. He took another sip of smoke and let it dribble out of his mouth as he talked. "They're supposed to represent us—the General Court and the Governor and his Council and all—but you put a man on top and the next thing you know he figures he's got a *right* to be on top, and that everybody else is supposed to do what he says. They even begin to figure that they have a right to own all the property, too. It's like you read about in the history books when they were all either lords or servants."

"It's not right for them to take our farms away to keep for themselves," I said.

"It doesn't matter if it's right or not," Levi said. "It's human nature, and you can't change human nature."

"That's not what our minister says," Tom said. "He says people should study to be good. He says people can improve themselves if they want."

Levi puffed a bit on his pipe. "I never met anybody I thought was improved. They all look pretty much like the same old model to me. You can't make a master not want to be a master, or a rich man give up his wealth. Look at Major Mattoon. You went against him and what happened? He gave you a smack across your tail or he set you out in the cold without anything but the clothes on your back."

"Well, if I'm bad I deserve it," Tom said.

I thought about Major Mattoon. "Levi's right," I said. "Mattoon never paid any attention to me. He just ordered me around like I was a mule. I mean, it didn't matter if I was right or not, he made me do what he wanted, no matter what."

"That's it," Levi said. "It's the same with the government. Your father or Peter or whoever you've got for master wants you to do what you're told and no rebelliousness, and it doesn't matter what's right."

"What Molly says is that Peter's got the responsibility for

us all. He has to be the master so he can see that things run right."

"Well sure, if you're talking about little children," Levi said, letting the smoke dribble out of his mouth some more. "You can't let a little child run around and do anything he wants. Sooner or later he's bound to get trod on by a horse or get into poison ivy. But it's different with us because we're grown-ups. The government shouldn't try to treat grown-ups like little children, because the government is just grown-ups, too."

Levi was a pretty good arguer, that was for sure. "Then there wasn't any point in kicking out King George. If the General Court isn't going to do what we want either, we might as well have kept the British."

"No, you've got it the wrong way around. We don't have to keep either of them. We have to kick them both out. I mean that's what we're doing here today. And we should have done it at the last elections. If there's enough of us to beat 'em in battle, there sure was enough of us to elect our people to the General Court. We were stupid not to send our representatives. The British tried to run us around like a herd of cattle, so we kicked them out. Now the new government is taxing us to death and putting us in prison and when we ask for new laws so we can keep our farms and feed our families, why they tell us to shut up." He sucked up the last of the smoke in his pipe, knocked the ashes into his hand, and threw them out into the snow where they wouldn't set the hay on fire. "I mean, after all, Just, why are you fighting? What are you here for?"

I was glad it was sort of dark in the barn because the question made me blush. I wasn't there to stand up for our rights so much as to make myself a hero. I felt ashamed. I wasn't out for the good of all of us, I wasn't out to save poor farmers from losing their land. I was thinking about getting to be a hero. I was out for myself.

Yet the funny thing was I didn't believe that Levi was out for the poor farmers, either. I didn't have any reason for believing that, it was just a feeling I had. I tried to think of a way to say it without being insulting. "Well, listen, Levi. Why are *you* here? I mean, did you come to fight to save the poor farmers from getting thrown in debtors' prison?"

"Partly. My father can't pay his taxes either," he said. "I'm here to keep the government from pushing me around."

"You're out for yourself, then."

"I sure am," he said. "I told you, that's human nature. It's human nature for the rich to want to stay rich, and the poor to want to get rich and for the ones on the top to push on the ones below, and it's human nature for the ones on the bottom to push back. I'm just going according to my human nature."

Levi Bullock sure was a good arguer. But I wasn't sure he was right. I didn't want to get rich or powerful. I just wanted to keep what was mine, and not have anybody lording it over me. I was determined I was going to think about the whole thing before I said anything else.

Chapter Ten

 FOR THE NEXT FEW DAYS WE JUST HUNG around Pelham. Nobody felt very good. It seemed like Lincoln had four thousand men to our two thousand. On top of it, they all had good Brown Bess muskets with bayonets, and some cannons, too. We didn't see how we could beat them unless we got awfully lucky. It just seemed like we were doomed to get beaten, with a lot of us getting killed for nothing. But we didn't have much choice about it. If we just gave up, they would go right ahead taking our farms away and putting us in jail. And of course those of us who were fighting might be put in prison or even get hanged, for being rebellious, although I didn't see how they could hang all two thousand of us. We felt like we were in a trap. There didn't seem to be any way out.

Of course, anyone who wanted to could quit and take the oath of allegiance. A few did—maybe four or five. None of the rest of us would speak to them. They had to leave Pelham. Most of us stuck it out, if only because we didn't want to go against our friends and neighbors.

On Wednesday I went out to the farm to see Molly. It had only been ten days since I'd seen her, but so much had happened that it seemed like a year. I felt as if I was a different person—more grown up or something. I gave her a hug. "Well," she said, "You don't look too bad."

"I guess I'm all right," I said. "Sort of hungry, though. There's never enough to eat."

"It's a surprise that there's anything at all. Everybody in Pelham has been giving as much as they could for the troops, but it isn't near enough. I spent the past three days collecting what I could. I borrowed a sleigh and a horse from Uncle Billy and went around to the farms. Most of the people are willing to help, but they don't have much to give."

"With all the rain and sleet I don't see how you got through."

"Oh, I managed somehow. But if we get too much more snow a lot of the roads will be shut off," she said.

"What do you think's going to happen?" I asked.

"I don't know," she said. "I haven't seen Peter for a couple of days, but he doesn't know much anyway. Nobody does. Not even General Shays."

"Do you think there'll be killing?"

"There usually is in war," she said.

I wondered what she would do if I got killed, but I didn't want to talk about that. She gave me some bread and milk, and then I walked back to the barn. Seeing her made me feel a little better, but still there was a lot of gloom everywhere.

On Thursday, which was the first of February, it snowed three more inches. We began to get rumors that we were going to move. I asked Peter about it once when we were at the tavern getting provisions. "I don't know," he said. "I wouldn't tell you if I did, anyway. There are too many rumors going around as it is." But on Saturday we got the order to form up. Nobody was happy about that, because it was snowing again. We didn't know why we were moving. All we knew was that we formed up and headed out on the road northeast to Petersham. We had a lot of sleighs and pungs going along with us to haul our provisions in—sacks of cornmeal; great hunks of salted, smoked hams and beef; barrels of molasses, rum, and cider; a few live pigs with their feet tied so they couldn't run off; and some turkeys and chickens in sacks.

Oh, the snow was terrible. They had put some men out front on horseback dragging logs along the road to flatten the snow down. Otherwise, we wouldn't have been able to get through at all. Some of the men were able to find places to ride on the sleighs, but most had to walk. It was a pretty miserable trip, with everybody wet and cold and on top of it scared that Lincoln was coming along behind us and might burst out on us at any moment. But he didn't, and by the end of the day we were in Petersham, bedded down in barns all over town. It was pretty cozy in the barn. The snowstorm had turned into a blizzard, and that meant that Lincoln wouldn't be able to get to us: Nobody was going to come out in a blizzard. Besides there was no way to get into Petersham but through a deep, narrow gorge between two rugged hills—and up a nearly vertical cartway—full of snow. We didn't even bother to put out a night watch. There was no need for it.

In the morning I sat down with Tom and Levi and we

shared what we had for breakfast—a little bread and some cheese, mostly. The snowstorm had stopped. It was cold and windy. We were sitting there eating when we heard the sound of a horse outside.

"Somebody must be mighty cold, riding in weather like this," Tom said.

"Sounds like more than one," I said. We heard a shout. The men in the barn looked up. There was another shout, and more sounds of horses. One of the men near the door got up and pushed it open a crack. He stared for a couple of seconds and then he slammed the door shut and bolted it. "God Almighty," he said. "It's Lincoln's army."

"It can't be," somebody cried. "Not in this weather." There came a pounding on the door, a hammering, and then a ripping, splintering sound. A board flew off the door and a bayonet slashed through. Our men were up now and swirling around the barn. "Out the back," somebody shouted. "There are windows in the back."

We raced through the gloom of the barn—Levi, Tom, and I. Behind us there came a huge crash. I spun around. The door flapped open, a mess of broken boards. The soldiers were piling through, bayonets fixed. "Don't move, anybody," one of them shouted.

We hit the back windows. There were three of them, about four feet off the floor, which had been covered with cloth. The men were diving through head first into the snow outside. Behind us there was an enormous crash of gunfire. It sounded as if it had gone off right at our backs. I went through a window and dropped into the snow-covered barnyard outside. It was a mess there. Some of our men were trying to hitch up pungs and sleighs, so as to get away with our provisions if they could. I struggled to my feet, and as I did so a bunch of horsemen charged into the barnyard waving swords and pistols. The men trying to get horses hitched to the sleighs just broke and ran.

Lincoln's horsemen began racing around the barnyard trying to run our men down. There were a couple of sheds off to the left and right, and a rail fence that joined the sheds to the barn to make a complete circle. Out beyond the fence was a field deep in snow. The only way we could get out was to run right through the riding men.

"Let's go," Levi said. We broke away from the side of the barn and charged forward. There was a horseman straight ahead of me. When he saw me coming he wheeled his horse around to face me, his sword raised. I ran straight at him and then at the last minute ducked around the horse on the side away from his sword. He made a swing at me, but I was already past. There was another horseman ahead. I ran straight for him too, and then shot off at an angle. He couldn't get his horse around quick enough to get in a swing at me.

Ahead of me was the barnyard fence. Another horseman sped by in front of me. I ducked back, but he was chasing somebody else. Then, just a few yards ahead, I saw lying in the muddy snow of the barnyard a musket, a good Brown Bess from the Revolutionary War. I leaped forward, snatched it off the snow, flung it over the fence, and swung myself up on the top rail. To one side I could see Levi going over the fence, too. I dropped down onto the crusted snow and sank in above my knees. I struggled up onto the crust and looked around. Tom was coming over the fence. I snatched up the musket, and the three of us began to slog through the snow across the field. We were able to walk on the crust, but there were eight to ten inches of fresh snow on top of the crust and it was hard going. The horsemen couldn't follow us into the snow. As long as they didn't decide to settle down in the barnyard and start shooting at us we'd be all right. A couple of times I looked back. There were a lot of men going across the field with us, men running down the road that went by the barn, men going every which way that you could see. The whole Regulator army was scattering. We'd run again.

Ahead, there was a hill with a woodlot on top. We just naturally went toward that. By the time I came up there were already a dozen or so men crouched at the edge of the woods, breathing hard and staring back down at the barn and the scattering army.

Finally, there were about twenty men gathered there. We just stood there watching. Lincoln's troop had got a group of maybe thirty Regulators rounded up on the road, and were getting ready to march them back down the road toward Pelham under guard. There were no bodies lying in the barnyard that anybody could see. It didn't seem as if anyone had got killed. We all watched and finally somebody said, "That's it. It's over now."

"We don't know that yet," somebody else said.

"Huh," the first one snorted. "The whole army's scattered, and they've got the sleighs with all our provisions. I doubt if we've got enough ball and power to make a stand even if we had the chance."

Nobody said anything about that. We hadn't made a stand anywhere yet.

"What I can't figure is how they were able to come up on

us like that. It plain doesn't seem possible for them to ride all night through that kind of a blizzard."

"Wasn't possible, but they did it. The next question is what do we do now?"

Nobody knew. There was a lot of talk, with different ideas offered. Some were for giving up and going home in hopes that the General Court would pardon us. Some said there was too much risk of getting hanged if we did that. Others were for trying to find where Daniel Shays was. The talk went around; there was no conclusion. One thing was clear, though: we had to move on. Lincoln's troops would be scouring the neighborhood for Regulators. There was only one direction to move in. That was west. The farther west we went, the farther we were from Boston and the government. More important, the towns in the western part of Massachusetts had been strong for the Regulators all along. Levi and Tom both were from out there and had told me about it. Besides, just beyond was New York State, where the Massachusetts government couldn't touch us. "We probably ought to head for Pittsfield," somebody said. "I judge we'd be among friends there."

So we began to walk. Now I had the musket to carry as well as the sword. I was glad to have the musket, but it was awkward to carry. I couldn't keep both my hands in my pockets for warmth, but had to keep one on the musket. I waited until the outside one got cold, then I'd switch the musket over to my other shoulder and use my other hand for a while.

It was a good fifty miles to Pittsfield. I'd never been that far away from home in my life. I should have been excited, but I wasn't. Mainly I felt what everybody else felt—as

down as we could be. We'd lost, and we hadn't made a fight
of it. If you run once, you feel like a coward and get down
about it, but you figure you can make it up on the next
chance. But if you run again, you start to believe that
you're a coward in your soul and will never get over it. I
didn't like that feeling at all, and as we walked through the
woods and out across the next field I began to make ex-
cuses for myself. After all, we'd been taken by surprise.
There wasn't much way we could have fought the way
they'd jumped on us so sudden. Of course, we should have
put out a night watch, but who would have figured they
could get through a blizzard like that, especially at night?
Besides, we were outnumbered—at least that was what
everybody said. So when you added it all up, there wasn't
much we could have done except run. But no matter what
I told myself, I still felt sick and downhearted that I'd run
away once again.

For the first few miles of the trip westward we stayed off
the roads, where Lincoln's men might be looking for Regulators. We cut across fields and stayed in woods and hol-
lows as much as we could. A group of twenty men going
through the countryside was pretty conspicuous. But after
we'd got through New Salem, Shutesbury, and into
Leverett, we figured we were safe from Lincoln's men for
the time being anyway, and began using the roads. That
was a relief, because the snow in the roads had been worn
down and we could go along pretty easy. In the fields we
had been wading in snow and, of course, the legs of our
trousers had been wet all the time and frozen stiff as fence
rails sometimes, too.

We walked all day Sunday and slept in the barn of a

friendly farmer that night, and walked all the next day, too. As we went along, we would stop at farmhouses along the way and ask for food. None of the people had very much to give, but usually they'd find something—a couple of loaves of bread or some cheese or maybe some dried apples. It was enough to keep us going, but I was pretty hungry a lot of the time.

We stopped at taverns to ask for help, too. They'd give us rum and water to warm us up. More important than the rum, though, was the news you always learned at taverns. Of course, a lot of it was just rumors. It was hard to know exactly what to believe. But generally when we got the same information from two or three different places we trusted it. What we found out was that things were pretty desperate, but that it wasn't over yet. General Shays and some of the other leaders had gone north to Vermont, where they'd be safe, unless the Vermont government decided to throw them out. The Massachusetts government had put out a reward of one hundred and fifty pounds for General Shays and a hundred pounds for the other leaders. Governor Bowdoin had issued a new clemency proclamation. Any of us, except the officers, who turned in our weapons and took the oath of allegiance would be pardoned. But he wouldn't be allowed to vote or teach school or run an inn for three years after. We also heard that a lot of Regulators were gathering down in Berkshire County, right on the New York border. Nobody knew who was there, or what their plans were, but we believed the story, because Berkshire County was pretty solid for our side and would be a logical place for Regulators to go to.

We debated about what to do. Some people thought it made better sense to accept the Governor's clemency—turn in the weapons and be pardoned. But most didn't. Some didn't trust the government—we might turn in our guns and then they'd jail us anyway. Others wanted to fight on. I was torn. I was having a pretty miserable time of it—cold, hungry, wet, and tired most of the time. But still, I hated to quit as a coward. And I thought that if there were Regulators in Berkshire County, I might have one more chance to do something brave. Levi and Tom were sticking, and it would be hard for me to quit—what would they think of me? In the end, I decided to go out there. There was strength in numbers, somebody said.

We went on walking. We were making pretty poor time, partly because of having to stop to forage for food so much, and partly because of the weather. On February 8th, which was four days after we'd run from the barn in Petersham, we had a huge snowstorm—eight inches of snow in one day—and it went on snowing for three days after. We spent most of that time holed up in a barn being hungry. Then came a thaw, with warmer weather for a few days, and we began walking again, first through Pittsfield and then south through Berkshire County, trying to track down the Regulators who were supposed to be there. Then more bad weather—rain, snow, sleet, and always cold. And finally, somewheres a bit south of Pittsfield, we heard that there was a pretty good-sized bunch of Regulators across the border in New York State, in a town called New Lebanon. So we walked across the border.

We stopped at a tavern for advice, and the innkeeper

said, "There's a big fellow who seems to be one of the leaders. A fellow with a fierce temper who's spoiling to have a crack at the government troops. He's likely to be up here this evening looking for news and something to drink."

My heart lifted. "That's Peter," I said to Levi. "It's got to be."

"How can you be sure?"

"I'll bet on it," I said. "I'd bet anything on it."

And I was right. I hung around the tavern all afternoon and into evening, and about eight o'clock Peter came stumping in, slapping his arms across his shoulders to beat off the cold. I was sitting in a corner so as to be out of the way, and he walked right past me.

"Peter," I cried.

He swung around as if he'd been smacked from behind, and the next thing I knew he had me clear off the ground and was hugging me and shouting out, "Justin, you've sprung out of the air again. How on earth did you ever find your way here?"

It was nice being back with Peter again. He got us each a glass of rum and water, and I told him the story—about how we'd been run out of the barn and how we walked all the way there and the rest of it. He'd walked there, too, he told me. Lincoln's troops took Brother at Petersham.

"What's going to happen?" I asked him, after I'd let that news sink in. "Are we still fighting?"

Peter grinned. "I think so. Daniel Shays has gone up to Vermont and he doesn't dare come back because they'll hang him sure if they catch him. A lot of the other men have given up and gone home. But I don't think it's over yet. There's a fellow here named Perez Hamlin—Captain Hamlin, he is. He's got a scheme in mind and I'm backing him on it."

"What is it?" I asked.

"You'll know in a few days, if we can get it going."

That was all he would say about it. The next morning I discussed it with Tom and Levi in the barn. We sat in a cart that was stored there. The light filtered down through cracks in the walls and roof so we could see each other in the gloom pretty well. Somebody had given Levi a little tobacco, about enough for three pipefuls, and he was smoking. "What I heard was that most of Lincoln's militia are going home," he said. "The General Court only voted them enough pay for three months, so they're quitting."

"You mean that Lincoln doesn't have his army anymore?"

"Oh, he's probably got some, and you can bet that the Governor will send more out. But right now they're mostly gone."

"Where did you hear that, Levi?" I said.

"Somebody in the tavern was talking about it. It wasn't any secret that the militia were only called up for three months—it was in the newspapers."

It turned out that Levi was right. A few days later, Peter came down and told us about it. "Lincoln's left naked," he said. "He hasn't got more than a hundred troops with him. There'll be more coming, but for now he's got nobody. We think we can capture him. Then the shoe will be on the other foot. So see to your weapons. I think we're going to see some real fighting at last."

Chapter Eleven

EARLY ON THE MORNING OF MONDAY, FEBRU-
ARY 26, we marched out of New Lebanon and
across the border back into Massachusetts. There
were about a hundred of us. It was cold again,
good and cold, and the sky was dark and low. It was going
to snow again. I was pretty nervous. I'd stuffed a piece of
cloth in the barrel of my musket to keep it dry in case it
snowed again, and I checked it to make sure that it hadn't
fallen out. We didn't do much talking. I guess Levi and
Tom were as nervous as I was, although, of course, you
could never tell that by looking at Levi. He just walked
along as calm as could be, as if he were out for a Sunday
stroll. But I figured that was mostly show.

Peter was in good spirits, though. He was riding up and
down the marching line, shouting out cheerful things—
about how Lincoln was going to get his tail clipped this
time, and how we'd finally show them that the Regulators
could put up a good fight when they had the chance. It was
encouraging to listen to Peter talk like that. It raised your
spirits. But still, I was pretty nervous.

Once we got across the border, we began to head south in the direction of Stockbridge, and by noon we were marching into the village. Stockbridge had a large green, with a couple of taverns on one side of it and some houses down the other. The green was deep in snow, but the streets were pretty well packed down. People stood in the windows of houses, or came to their doors to watch us. We marched around the green and halted. Captain Hamlin broke us up into detachments of twenty men each. One detachment was sent out to round up food and other provisions, one was sent out to round up some of the leading men in the village as hostages.

I didn't understand it. "I thought everybody around here was with us," I said to Levi.

"I expect most of them are," he answered. "Leastwise, up in my part of the country they are."

"Then why are we stealing stuff and taking hostages?"

Levi shrugged. "There's always a few people in every town who'll truckle to government."

It didn't seem like a very good answer to me, but I didn't have a chance to argue with Levi about it because my detachment was sent off to find some horses and sleighs to carry the provisions in. We found two sleighs sitting in front of a tavern on the green. It was the biggest inn I'd ever seen in my life, called The Red Lion. We put a couple of men to guard the sleighs, and then the rest of us went out back to the tavern barn, untied two horses, and took them back out front to the sleighs. We were hitching them to the sleighs when the tavern owner came out. "Please, boys," he cried, "I need those horses to bring in my goods. I can't run my business without them."

"Sorry," somebody said. "We can't run our business without them, either." Some people came out of the tavern and stood in the yard, watching.

"Boys, I beg you. There are others around who can spare them better than me."

"Oh, they'll be making their contributions, too."

I felt sorry for the man. I didn't like stealing the horses, even if we had to. We got the horses hitched up to the sleigh. The man from the tavern went on begging. "Please, boys, we're all with you fellows, here."

"That's fine. Then you'll be happy to lend us your horses."

We led the horses and sleighs back around the green to where Captain Hamlin was waiting with some others. There were a dozen men standing there, shivering and looking scared. They were the hostages. I wondered who they were.

Men began to come in with provisions—sacks of corn-meal, barrels of cider, sides of pork. We loaded up the sleighs, formed up, and set out, still heading south. We were heading for Great Barrington, where there were a lot of farmers in prison for debt. I felt guilty about taking the hostages and the horses, but it felt good for us to be on top for a change. The men were in good spirits—we'd really done something, finally.

We got down to Great Barrington toward the end of the afternoon. There was a snow-covered green here, too, with taverns and houses around it. We marched around the green and halted. People stood at doors and windows and watched us, nervous about what we might do. At one window in a house near to where I was standing two little children were looking out a window. All I could see were their faces with big eyes peering out. I figured it was something they'd remember all their lives, and it made me proud to be part of it. It made me feel the glory in it.

Peter took a detachment down a side lane that led away from the green. In about fifteen minutes they came back leading a bunch of ragged-looking men. The men ran cheering into the streets. They were the ones who'd been jailed for debt. They spread out in all directions and disappeared. I figured they were heading for their homes.

It was beginning to get dark. Peter came down the line and broke us into groups of ten. Each group got a ration of food and then went off to spend the night in barns. I was tired from all that marching, and I slept pretty well. When I woke up in the morning, Peter was shaking me. "What?" I said, sitting up in the gloom of the barn.

"Get up," he said. He was crouched on his haunches in front of me. I rubbed my eyes. He looked me in the face. "Are you ready for a fight?"

I blinked and stared back. I was only half awake. "What?"

"You don't have to go if you don't want. You boys can change your minds if you want."

"What fight, Peter?"

"There are government troops out looking for us. A group of about a hundred or so. They've come out from Pittsfield after us."

I was a lot more awake now. Levi and Tom were sitting up in the hay, too, listening. "Are they coming here?" I asked.

Peter looked around at Levi and Tom, and then back to me. "We're not going to run anymore. We're going out to meet them. There'll be real fighting before the day is over, for sure. If you boys want to get out, now's the chance. Nobody would blame you. Nobody wants to see boys get killed."

My heart was whirring, and my stomach went cold. "I'm coming," I said.

Peter looked at Tom and Levi. "And you boys?"

"I'm coming."

"Me, too."

Peter stood up. "I hope we're all not sorry later. All right, form up by the green." And he went out.

Saying you are going out to meet the enemy and actually doing it are two different things. First you have to find him, and then you have to maneuver yourself around so you can take him from a good position. You want to catch him by surprise, or take him from a hilltop where there's good cover. And, of course, he'd be trying to do the same thing to us.

This meant an awful lot of marching to and fro at a pretty good clip. First Captain Hamlin would send out little detachments of two or three scouts in different directions. They'd try to find out from farmers or anybody else if the government troops had been by, and which direction they were going in. Then, when we got some information, we'd take off in the right direction. After we'd gone a ways and Captain Hamlin figured the enemy might be somewhere around, he'd send out some more scouts. So first we'd march at about as fast a pace as we could go, and then we'd stand around and wait while the scouts were out. I couldn't decide which was worse. I was always glad to stop marching and rest, but after we'd be standing around for a half hour in the cold, I'd start wishing we'd march again so I could get warm.

We did that all day, and at nightfall we were at a place called Egremont, which was on the New York State border. As it got dark, we drew rations and crawled into barns to sleep.

That was Tuesday. When we got up Wednesday morning it was snowing and we knew we were going to be cold and miserable all day. We ate breakfast quickly. Captain Hamlin had got information that the government troops were somewhere down near Sheffield, a town on the Connecticut border in the southwest corner of Massachusetts. He had heard that they were moving up toward Egremont to find us. We formed up and headed south in the direction of Sheffield. It seemed sure that the two enemies would bump into each other now. I just hoped they didn't catch us by surprise. With snow pouring down, our scouts wouldn't be able to see more than fifty yards ahead. The government troops could be marching right for us, and neither of us would know it until we were within close shooting distance of each other.

We marched all morning and at noon we found a barn and rested and then we went out to march again. The country we were going through now was very hilly. We kept going through ravines with steep, rocky cliffs going up on either side of us, and then up steep hills. Sometimes the road would be pure rock where ledges broke through the ground. There were great hemlocks everywhere. The land was too rocky for growing anything and too steep for cattle to graze. Some of these places had never been cleared; they'd been hemlock forests way back into Indian times. The hemlock forests were beautiful. The long branches of the trees stuck out straight so that there was a lot of room around each one. There was snow all over the branches, which made a kind of roof over the forest floor. The forests were filled with green light that the falling snow flickered through. It was beautiful, and it felt funny to think of war going on in a place so beautiful.

Still we marched, and still no government troops. The scouts were out permanently now; two in the front, two behind, and one on each side, working his way through the rocks and cliffs beside us. But the scouts weren't going to do much good. In the falling snow they wouldn't see the enemy much before the rest of us would.

Uphill and downhill through the craggy ravines and hemlock forests we went. And we were at the top of the hill going through a hemlock forest with its great tree trunks, wide spaces, and snow ceiling, when we heard a shout, and then a shot. "Halt," Captain Hamlin shouted. I saw the scouts come running toward us through the falling snow. "Take cover on both sides of the road," Hamlin shouted. Our line broke like a dropped glass as the men scattered, falling flat at the side of the road, or crouching down in the deep snow behind the hemlocks. I didn't even think. I just jumped in behind a tree trunk and crouched there, up to my knees in snow, my heart pounding like thunder.

There were more shots from up front, first a few, and then a steady fusillade. Balls whistled around me, thunking into tree trunks, or slashing through branches to send down cascades of snow. The government troops couldn't see us, but they knew where we were and they were firing randomly to keep us pinned down.

I kept my head behind the tree. I knew that sooner or later I would have to look out, but I was scared that the minute I did, I would catch a ball in my face. I looked around. I was about five yards off the road. Levi was off to one side of me behind a tree. I couldn't see Tom. There were other men behind trees, peeking around the trunks with their muskets aimed forward. Out in the road, two men lay on their faces. One of them was snaking his body over to the side of the road where there was better cover. The other one was not moving. Then I saw a kind of deep shudder pass over his whole body. He began to suck in air in deep gasps. I knew he was dying and I wondered what he was thinking.

I had to stop being a coward and get my face around the tree. I crouched as low as I could into the snow and began to peek around. Suddenly I remembered that the cloth was still in the muzzle of my musket. I pulled back and jerked the cloth out. Then I swung myself over so I could see around the tree.

There was nothing out there but hemlocks and falling snow. I realized that I was at the front of our line. I kept staring forward. In the distance through the falling snow I could see flashes of movement, but it was hard to make out what they were or how far away they were.

Now Peter came running up the road from the direction of the enemy. I guessed he had crawled in close to have a look at them. He was running crouched as low as he could, with his musket dangling in one hand. The firing suddenly got heavier and I could see balls kick up snow around him. He kept running until he was abreast of where we were crouched behind the trees and then he flung himself down in the road, with only his head raised up.

"Hold your fire, boys," he shouted. "Save your ammunition. They'll charge us soon. Stand firm, pick your targets, and wait until you've got a sure shot before you fire. We're as strong as they are. Stand firm and we can break the charge." Then he jumped up into the running crouch again and raced off to give his order to another bunch.

I pulled back behind the tree, took my father's sword out of its scabbard, and stuck it in the snow where I could grab it easily. I sure didn't like the idea of fighting a man who had a bayonet when I had only a sword. I didn't know anything at all about sword fighting. I opened up my powder and ball pouches. I didn't know if I'd have time to reload after I'd got off my first shot, but I wanted to be ready anyway.

I put myself far enough around the tree to point my musket forward and fire. The man lying in the road was still gasping for breath. Every once in a while that deep shudder would pass over him. My heart was pounding and my head was numb. I couldn't think. All I knew was that in a few minutes I would either kill a man or be killed myself, and I knew that I didn't want to do either. Waiting was awful. I didn't want them to come, I wanted them suddenly to march off in the other direction. But the waiting was so bad half of me wanted them to come to get it over with.

Then, through the falling snow I saw movement. There came a shout in the woods, and then another one, and at last I saw men, real men, running up the road toward us, their bayonets fixed on their weapons. They were forty or fifty yards down the road, brown blurs in the falling snow. I figured they wouldn't try to run through the deep snow in the woods, but would come up the road until they were abreast of us, and then make their charge into the woods.

There seemed like an awful lot of them. They filled the road. "Wait," I whispered to myself. "Wait, don't fire yet." I could make out their faces now, just the faces of ordinary men, the same kind of men I knew in my own troop, wearing the same kind of homespun clothes that we had on. Suddenly they veered off the road into the woods and spread out. They crouched down in the snow behind the trees the way we were, and began to fire. I ducked back behind my tree. The balls were thunking around us, but this time they could see us. I knew I had to look out again, because somebody could be charging silently through the snow at me. I put my face out and then swung my musket around. Then there was a shout, and they rose up from behind the trees and began running as fast as they could through the snow toward us. It looked like a forest of bayonets coming toward me. I blinked and made myself choose a man to shoot at. He was young, maybe eighteen or twenty, with a lot of blond hair sticking out of his cap, and he came and took one hand off his musket and wiped perspiration from his face. I just crouched there thinking, "How can I shoot him?" and the next thing I knew I was standing up with the musket to my shoulder. I let off one wild shot and turned and ran back through the hemlock forest, struggling through the snow away from those bayonets. I realized I'd run again.

I made myself stop and drop down behind a hemlock. I crouched there hating myself, cold from fear and hot from running. Around me everything was confusion. The government men were coming forward in little dashes, and our men were falling back, firing, and falling back again. There wasn't much they could do against those bayonets but retreat and try to reload on the run so they could fire again.

And then I saw Peter. He was standing in the middle of the road, right next to the body of the man who was dying. He was holding his musket over his head like a club.

Charging toward him was a government man, his bayonet thrust forward. Peter swung. The man swiveled sideways, but the barrel caught him on one shoulder. He dropped to one knee, and in one motion rose again, slicing upward with the bayonet. Peter jumped back. His left foot came down on the back of the dying man. Peter began to tip over backward, waving his arms as if he could somehow swing himself up again, and then he was lying on his back and the government man was jumping over the dying man to get at Peter.

I was halfway out of the forest before I even knew that I was moving, struggling desperately in the deep snow. Now the government man was over Peter, the bayonet poised. I plunged the last two steps out of the forest onto the cleared road. The government man pulled the bayonet back. I grabbed my musket by the barrel with both hands and flung myself forward. The government man started to jab. I swung the musket around like a club. It caught him on the side of his head. He shouted something, staggered off to the side of the road, and dropped to his knees. Peter leaped to his feet. I dashed back into the woods where I had come from, and Peter dashed off in the opposite direction into the woods across the road.

At that moment there came a drumming of gunfire from somewhere down the road. There were more government troops coming up the hill. There wasn't any hope anymore, and I began to run off through the forest as fast as I could go in the snow, heading away from the field of battle.

Chapter Twelve

I WASN'T ALONE. THERE WERE A LOT OF US struggling through the snow. We weren't headed in any direction, just away. Behind us were a lot of government troops with those fearsome bayonets. We were just fleeing in all directions. I kept on moving and finally up ahead, I made out Levi Bullock, standing against a tree and catching his breath. "Levi," I shouted.

He turned to face me and shook his head grimly. I came up. "We bit off more than we could chew that time," he said.

"At least we stood for a while," I said. I didn't like remembering that I'd run.

"Well, we did. But they were too many for us."

"Have you seen Tom Mayo?" I asked.

"He's up ahead somewhere. We'd better keep moving."

The government troops weren't following us, however. The snow was deep and it would be dark soon. "I guess they're content to scatter us," I said.

"They took some prisoners," Levi said. "I saw them

rounding up a bunch of our men on the road. It'll go hard with them."

I hoped they hadn't caught Peter. "Will they hang them?"

"They might," Levi said. "We'd better keep moving, at least until it's really dark."

We moved off, and shortly after that we came upon Tom Mayo, crouched in the snow, resting. There were still a few of our men scattered here and there in the forest, but with the dark coming it was hard to know how many. We stood in the snow, planning. "We've got to hide out for a while," Levi said. "Nobody knows what the government might do to punish us."

"But where?"

"I think we ought to go up to Lanesboro," Levi said. "My family will hide us until we can find out what the government intends to do."

"It'll be risky anyplace we go," I said. "If we'd have given up and taken the oath after Petersham like some of the others did, we'd be free and clear, but they're not likely to give us pardons now—not after taking those hostages and opening the jail at Great Barrington."

"That's the point," Levi said. "If they punish anybody, it'll be us."

"Lanesboro's for the Regulators," Tom said.

"If they send the sheriff after us it won't matter who Lanesboro is for," Levi said. "But I can't think of a better place to go."

Levi was right—Lanesboro was the best idea. It sure wouldn't have been smart for me to take a chance on getting back to Pelham. It'd take me a week to walk there, with government soldiers and sheriffs all around. We could get to Lanesboro in a couple of days. "We should go to Lanesboro and rest up a little, anyway. The main thing is that we've got to get out of these woods pretty quick. We can't spend the night here. We'd freeze to death. We've got to find a barn." It crossed my mind that maybe I'd never get back to Pelham, but would spend my life wandering from village to village dodging the sheriffs.

We started off, cutting through the woods away from the road in hopes of coming upon another road somewhere. Finally the hemlocks gave out. We broke into an open field and soon enough came down onto a road. We walked along a few miles until it was dead night and most people would be asleep, and then we snuck into the first barn we came to and bedded down in the hay for the night. We got up at dawn and began walking again. Every once in a while we came to a fork in the road. We never knew which fork to take, but Levi said that if we kept heading in a northerly direction, sooner or later we'd hit some place he'd recognize. We walked all day, skirting around little villages through the fields when we came to them. We were cold and tired and wet and hungry, but we'd been all of those things for weeks and we knew that the best thing was to try not to think about them, and keep up a cheerful conversation. By nightfall Levi began to recognize the roads, and by midnight we were in Lanesboro.

The Bullocks certainly made a fuss over us. Of course, they'd never heard of me and Tom before, but they were so happy to have Levi home, safe and sound, that they were glad to see us, too. They gave us a big meal of pork and gravy and cornbread and cider and then the question came up of where we should sleep.

"Word will get out sooner or later that you're here," Mr.

Bullock said. "But I doubt if anybody'll come after you tonight. You'll be all right sleeping in the house." So we slept inside, Levi in his own bed and me and Tom in front of the fire on some sacking. I didn't have any trouble getting to sleep.

I felt a lot better in the morning. Mrs. Bullock fed us with a good hot breakfast of fried meat, cornmeal mush, and molasses. I tell you, right then, dry clothes and a good hot meal seemed about as close to heaven as you could get. We sat there eating away and Mr. Bullock asked us a lot of questions about the battle. Levi told him his story, which was that his gun had misfired and he'd run off a ways into the woods to clear it when the second batch of government troops arrived and drove us off. Then he told his father my story—how I'd run out of the woods and knocked the militiaman down with my musket.

Mr. Bullock nodded. "That was very daring, Justin," he said. "It makes you the big hero of the event."

I couldn't believe what he was saying. "I wasn't so brave, sir," I said. "I ran when they started to charge."

He laughed. "Good Lord, boy, you risked your life going onto the road after that government man. If that fella had seen you coming, he'd have run you through."

I blushed. "I didn't think of that. I was just scared he'd kill Peter."

"Stop being modest, Just," Tom said. "Everybody saw what you did. I heard one man say that it was about the only brave thing he'd seen anybody do since the troubles began."

"That's right," Levi said. "You've got pretty near the only glory to come out of the whole thing."

It was so hard to believe. I'd been a hero at last without

even realizing it. It had been almost an accident. I hadn't *meant* to do anything glorious. I'd just done it to sa Peter, and now everybody thought I was a hero. I want to think about it some more.

But I couldn't think about it just then, because we had to decide what to do next. I wanted to get back to Pelham as soon as possible, but it would have been foolhardy to leave right away. It was a better idea to wait around for a day or so to see how the land lay.

In the afternoon, Mr. Bullock went up to the tavern and picked up the gossip. He told us, "Lincoln's got men all over the place. You fellows killed a couple of government men, and one of the hostages got killed, too, although nobody knows who shot him. School teacher named Solomon Gleazen. They'll be looking for anybody who was in the fight, at least for now. You're going to have to keep yourselves pretty well hidden, in case they send somebody out looking for you. People in Lanesboro know that Levi was off with Shays, and the justices might send the sheriff around just to check. I think you ought to sleep in the barn tonight. If anybody shows up, somebody will slip out and warn you. You can hide up in the woodlot until it's safe to come down."

So that was what we did. Around nine at night we went out to the barn and sat around talking for a while. Then we lay down to sleep. It seemed to me like I'd been sleeping in barns forever. It was pretty cold. There was a good wind blowing, and it cut through the cracks in the barn walls. It was hard getting to sleep. Finally Levi said, "Listen, I've got an idea. Let's sleep in the potato hole. It'll be warm as toast in there."

"Is there room?" Tom said.

"I think so," Levi said. "Anyway, it's a perfect place to hide. Nobody would think of looking for us there."

We followed Levi outside. The potato hole was dug into the slope of a hill above the barn. It went in diagonally to make a kind of cave. A lot of farmers had potato holes like the Bullock's. You stored things like apples and turnips and parsnips and of course potatoes in them in the winter. Being in a hole in the earth kept them the right temperature—not so warm that they'd rot, not so cold that they'd freeze.

The cover was a big square made of oak planking. It was pretty heavy. We pulled it off and had a look. There was enough moon so we could see inside pretty well. The hole was filled with sacks of vegetables and things. There wasn't much room left over. It would be nice and cozy, though, once our body heat warmed things up.

"Slide in and try it, Tom," Levi said.

Tom slid in and scrunched down among the sacks. "There's room for one more, but not for both of you," he said.

Levi looked at me. "I'll choose you for it, Just," he said.

"You'd better take it, Levi. If the sheriff comes around he'll know who you are, but he won't recognize me. He'll think I'm just some hired hand." To be honest, that wasn't my real reason for letting him have the potato hole. I was thinking that if I'd become a hero, I might as well go on acting like one.

"We should choose," Levi said.

"That's all right, I'll sleep in the barn." He shrugged and climbed down into the potato hole. They looked nice and cozy and warm down there, and I felt sort of sorry I wasn't with them. I heaved the cover over them. "Can you fellows breathe all right in there?"

"Sure," Levi said. "There's a few cracks between the planks.

"Are you sure? You might suffocate down there."

"I can feel cold air coming in on my hand if I put it up to the cracks," Levi said.

"All right," I said, and walked back to the barn. I snuggled down in the hay as best I could, but it took me a while to get to sleep. I kept thinking how cozy Tom and Levi must be. To get myself to sleep I began to think about being a hero and all that. What was a hero? Did it count if you didn't mean to do something heroic, but just did it? What about if you ran away first and then came back and did something glorious? Would being a hero and a coward cancel each other out? And didn't you have to be fighting for some glorious cause like God or liberty or something to be a hero? I mean, could you be heroic if you were just fighting against unfair taxes and laws that let rich men get the farms of poor men? I wanted to know. I wanted to know if I was really a hero or not. I mean, even if a lot of people called me a hero, did that really make me one? Maybe there weren't any heroes, just ordinary people who were cowards sometimes and heroes sometimes and most of the time just ordinary people.

Anyway, why did I worry about being a hero so much? Why did I want to be one? Maybe it would be better to forget about the whole hero problem and just go about my business like anybody else. I didn't know the answers, and after a while I went to sleep.

When I woke up, there was a vague light in the barn. It

felt like it was morning, but it was pretty dark. I stood up and looked out through the cracks in the barn door and saw that it was snowing pretty hard. It had been snowing for several hours. There was a good six inches of fresh snow over the old crust. It must be true what the old-timers were saying—it was the coldest, snowiest winter in a hundred and fifty years.

I stood there half awake, wondering if the snow had fallen through the cracks in the cover to the potato hole. It would have been pretty uncomfortable for Tom and Levi to have had snow trickling through all night. Then it occurred to me that the snow wouldn't do that. The first few flakes might filter through the cracks, but then it would begin to pile up, covering everything, cracks, planks, and all. The next thing I thought was, would the snow block off the air from coming through the cracks? I began to feel uneasy. Of course, they hadn't suffocated. There would certainly be enough air coming through somehow. Or if they began to suffocate, they would certainly wake up and push the cover open a crack to get more air. But did suffocating wake you up? Or could you suffocate in your sleep and die without even knowing it?

I swung the barn door open and jumped outside. The fresh snow was soft and dry and I plowed through it easily, sliding my feet along the crust underneath so as not to break through. I kept telling myself not to worry, they would be all right. In a couple of minutes I reached the potato hole. It was covered with six inches of snow, but you could tell where it was because the snow was raised a few inches in a square over the plank cover.

"Hey, Levi," I shouted.

There was no answer. Probably they couldn't hear me because of the snow. Maybe they were still asleep because it was so dark in there. I dropped to my knees and brushed the snow off the planking with my hands. "Hey, Levi. Hey, Tom."

There was no answer. In a minute the plank cover was clear of snow. I heaved on it, shoving it back. Now the hole was open.

They looked like they were asleep, all curled up together on the potato sacks, lying there so peaceful. But their eyes were open and they were staring straight ahead at nothing. I shrieked, "Oh my God," and ran down to the house.

They brought the bodies in and laid them out side by side on a trestle of planks and sawhorses. Then Mr. Bullock went out to the barn to make coffins. There would be a church service in a day or so, and then the burying. But I didn't stay. I couldn't. I was cold as death inside.

Chapter Thirteen

I WALKED ON HOME TO PELHAM BY THE shortest route, not skirting around towns or anything. I didn't care if I got caught or jailed or even hanged or anything. I just wanted to get home. All the way home I kept seeing my two friends curled up together in that hole, their eyes staring out. I tried not to see them, but I couldn't stop. The sight just kept coming up.

It took me five days to get home, sleeping in barns along the way and begging food where I thought people might be friendly to the Regulators. A lot of them were. Even though we'd lost, and most of the people who'd fought had taken the oath of allegiance, lots were still angry at the government. There was even some talk about getting some more fighting going again. I wasn't talking that way, though. I'd seen all the fighting I wanted to for a long while.

Of course, Molly fell all over me when I walked in the door. She'd had no idea where I'd been or whether I'd gotten killed, and she'd heard from Peter about me being a hero. "He said you saved his life. He said he was about to be stabbed with a bayonet and you ran out of the woods and knocked the man down."

"I wasn't really being brave," I said. "I was just scared for Peter."

"You're just being modest," she said. "I'm proud of you."

A week ago I'd have been happy to have her say that. But now, with that picture in my mind of those two fellows in the potato hole, it didn't matter very much anymore that I'd been a hero. What difference did it make when my friends were dead? How could I feel good about it?

"Where's Peter now?" I said.

"Northampton jail," she said.

"Jail?"

"They took him prisoner after the battle. He tried to escape along the road and ran smack into a whole bunch of government men. They cornered him up against a tree with their bayonets and beat him down with their muskets."

"He should have run off into the woods the way everybody else did."

"Of course he should have. But you know Peter. He was trying to rally the men to make one more stand."

"It was hopeless by then," I said.

"Peter never thinks anything is hopeless. You remember the Forlorn Hope Squad."

"Yes," I said. "What will happen to him now?"

She shrugged. "There's to be an indictment and then a trial, and of course he'll be found guilty of treason. Then it'll be up to the judge to pass sentence. There's a lot of feeling around that everybody will be pardoned in the end. They've captured maybe sixty that were in the Sheffield fight. Nobody thinks they'll dare hang them all. People figure that if the government hangs a lot of plain farmers just because they were in the Regulators, there'd be an even worse rebellion than before. People figure that the Governor won't want to stir things up all over again, just when they're beginning to calm down. They've won, what do they have to gain from raising the people's feelings again?"

"But has the Governor actually said he would pardon everybody?"

"No," she said. "They haven't said anything yet. But they won't—they'll let us worry for a while first."

Actually, they hadn't caught many Regulators, just the sixty they'd taken at Sheffield and a few others they'd captured here and there. They weren't trying to catch anybody else. The rest of us had gotten away with it, whether we'd taken the oath or not. It didn't seem fair. Why should these particular men have to suffer for what thousands of us had done? Even Daniel Shays and the other leaders were safe in Vermont. They weren't going to get into any trouble.

It was a pretty unhappy time for us. I kept having my memories of things: of the cannon fire at Springfield, of the race through the barnyard at Petersham, of the bayonet charge at Sheffield, and especially of Levi and Tom in the potato hole. I would dream about these things and wake up in a sweat at night, my heart going wild in my chest. One evening when I was out in the woodlot sawing wood, I suddenly fell down on my knees and burst into tears. I went on kneeling there and crying for a long time, and then I began to pray to God for Tom and Levi. After that the picture of them curled up in the potato hole got more dim and came to me less often, and I slept better.

But still it was an unhappy time. There was Peter in jail, and nobody knowing what would happen, and a terrible hard winter still not over, and the work. I'd worked hard before, but never as hard as now, with no Peter around. I went from before sun-up until after dark, and sometimes worked by candlelight at night, husking dry corn until my head would just droop over and I'd fall asleep on the hearth. And then have to start all over again the next day.

And of course we'd lost. But the funny thing about that was I didn't care very much. I couldn't figure that out. You'd have thought that after so much fighting and so much suffering it would feel awful to have it come to nothing. But the truth was, I didn't care. I was just glad that it was over, and wished we could get back to normal.

We had one big hope, though. On April 2nd there was going to be elections for a new General Court. It would be a chance for us to send our own sort of people to the government. We realized how stupid we'd been. Dozens of towns in our part of the state hadn't bothered to send representatives to the General Court for a long time. It had always seemed to be too expensive to send a man all the way over to Boston and pay all his expenses for weeks at a time. It seemed to everybody that it would just mean more taxes. So we didn't send anybody, and of course it ended up that we didn't have any say in what laws were passed. We could see now that if we'd had more sense and sent people—not just us, but all the towns in our part of the state—we'd have had a mighty big vote in the General Court. Most people figured we would have been able to pass at least some of the laws we wanted. It seemed likely that we'd never have had to fight. And Tom and Levi wouldn't be dead.

Of course, there was a lot of electioneering going on. There was talk about who'd be best for the job, and who ought to stand for election, and a lot of men were putting themselves forward for it. Over in Amherst, Major Mattoon was going to stand. He'd been in the General Court before, and it was natural for him to try again. I just wished I could vote in Amherst so I could vote against him; but I was too young to vote anywhere. It was a funny thing, but he didn't scare me the way he used to. After being through a bayonet charge, having somebody like him snap at you didn't seem very much. I started dropping the Major off his name and calling him Mattoon when I talked about him.

But important as the elections were, our main problem was Peter. All through March, Molly kept making trips over to Northampton to see him. I wanted to go, too, but I had to stay home and look after the little ones. Being as she was his wife, she had the right to go. She said they were treating Peter pretty well. The food was good, there were the other men to talk to, and she was allowed to bring him rum when she came to see him. And that awful winter was over. Spring came on and it was warm again—even in the jail. "But you know Peter," she said. "He can hardly stand being locked up. He gets into a rage sometimes and stands there shaking the bars as if he were going to break them out."

Then the trial came. The charge in the indictment said that Peter and the others

> . . . *with drums beating, fifes playing and with guns, pistols, bayonets, swords, clubs and divers other weapons . . . did assault, imprison, captivate, plunder, destroy, kill and murder divers of the leige subjects . . .*

They all pleaded not guilty, but the trial didn't last very long. Seventeen were declared guilty. The rest were let off. Out of all the people they caught, they picked only the ones who had taken a really prominent part in the fighting. The government did not dare hang a whole lot of plain farmers for fear that they'd have a worse rebellion on their hands. Most people around Pelham said they wouldn't even dare hang the seventeen they found guilty. Of course, Peter was one of the seventeen—with him riding out front on that big Brother at Springfield, and being involved in the killing at Sheffield and all, it just had to happen.

Now the question was: What kind of sentence would the judge give the guilty ones? We could only wait and find out.

Meanwhile, the elections were coming up. Being a woman, of course, Molly couldn't vote. It put her in a rage almost like the ones Peter got in. "Why can't I vote?" she would shout at me when we discussed it. "You'll be able to vote in a few years, but I'll never be able to vote. Do you think you're smarter than I am?"

"It's not my fault, Molly," I said. "If it was up to me, you could vote."

"Do you think you know more about who ought to run the government than I do? Why does some ignorant shoemaker who can hardly read have the right to vote when I can't? I know more than most of the men around here."

That was true: She was smarter than a lot of men I knew. Lots of them could hardly read or write. "If it was up to me, you could vote, Molly."

She calmed down. "I know it, Just. It makes me mad is all. I can't vote because I'm a woman, you can't vote because you're too young, Peter can't vote because he's in jail. With all the suffering this family has done for people's rights, we don't have a vote."

It didn't seem fair. Oh, Molly would go down to the tavern and speak her mind about it when discussions were being held as to who should stand for election. She said she had a right to speak out because Peter was in jail and couldn't speak for himself. They let her. They figured Peter might be angry at them if they didn't, and nobody wanted to be on his bad side when he got out of jail. She even tried to claim the right to Peter's vote, but she couldn't convince them of that. Once they let one woman vote, they'd all want to vote, they said. Voting was men's business, they said.

Finally election day came. The voting was held at the meeting house. I went over toward evening to see how it had come out. They were all pretty drunk. It was a big night. And when they counted the ballots, we found our man had won. Then, of course, we had to wait while the news gradually trickled in from the towns around. Eventually we found we'd won all over the state. In Amherst, Mattoon had lost. Not only did people on our side get a huge number of seats in the General Court, but Governor

Bowdoin was put out of office, too. In his place there was elected John Hancock, who'd been our governor before. Now, finally, we had hope that some of our grievances would be redressed. Thomas Johnson was sent to the General Court from Pelham. He'd been a Regulator, so he and all the others who'd been elected to town offices, even Uncle Billy, had to take an oath of loyalty to the government. It didn't go down so bad, they said, because all the towns around sent men who'd fought with Daniel Shays to represent them and now the Regulators would have their say about making the laws. Maybe they'd even be able to get all the prisoners like Peter pardoned.

But Peter was still in jail. Molly wrote up a petition asking the new governor to be merciful and pardon him, and sent it over to Boston. We waited. Finally on April 30th, the Governor's Council handed down their decision. Peter was sentenced to hang.

The strange part was that out of the seventeen who'd been found guilty, only six were going to be hanged—two men from Hampshire County, two from Berkshire County, one from Worcester County, and one from Middlesex County. The two from our county were going to be Peter and a man named Nathaniel Austin. The date was set for May 24th, three weeks away.

"They're just trying to make an example," Molly said. "They don't dare hang a lot of people for fear of stirring up another rebellion. But they want to hang a few just to show who is master. They only picked men from the most rebellious counties."

"But why Peter?"

She shrugged. "Who knows? I don't think it mattered to

them who they picked, so long as they have somebody to hang. Oh, they probably picked Peter because he stands out. He was always in the thick of things. He was up front at the Springfield Arsenal and he was at Petersham and he was one of the leaders at Sheffield where those two militiamen got killed. Everybody all around this part of the state knew about him."

"What are we going to do?"

"We can still hope that they'll pardon them all in the end."

But Molly wasn't the type to just hope. She went over to Northampton and came back with another woman—Nathaniel Austin's wife, Abigail. "We're getting up a petition," Molly said. "We're going to take it to Boston."

They got a man named Theodore Sedgewick to help them write it up. It was pretty fancy:

> *Let not! Oh let not! one rash action shut each avenue of mercy . . . acknowledge the impartiality of trial and sentence and recognize the error of our conduct . . . wholly ignorant of the rights of the constitution and privileges therein contained . . . unskilled in the true principles of government . . .*

It was a lot of stuff like that. We took it around town to get people to sign it. I took it over to the tavern one night. There were a lot of people willing to sign. In fact, pretty near everybody in town would have signed it if there'd been space enough at the bottom of the page. They all thought it was unfair for Peter and Nathaniel Austin to hang when practically everybody else around town had done the same things. A lot of people thought there would be trouble if the six men were hanged. "The old Regulators will rise up again if it happens," some said. But that wouldn't do Peter much good if he was already dead.

So Molly and Abby Austin borrowed some horses from Uncle Billy and rode all the way to Boston. It was an awful long, hard trip—it took three days. But Molly could do almost anything any man her size could. They finally got into the State House and gave the petition to the Governor's Council. It did some good, but not very much. They came back with a reprieve until June 21st. It said that they should be "hanged by the neck until dead between noon and three o'clock of that day." But Molly as always still had hope.

"What will we do now?" I asked her.

Molly was pretty grim. "Peter has to beg for mercy. He has to humble himself. I'm going to write a letter for him to sign." She wrote:

Feeling the deepest sorrow and remorse and in full knowledge of the evils of my conduct, I now admit great shame and guilt. But I was never an officer in the Regulators, but having a good horse and a foolish fondness to be thought active and alert I was persuaded to take an old cutlass and ride at the head of a column during the attack on the Springfield Arsenal. I had left home unarmed and was guilty merely of uttering foolish and wicked expressions for which I am deeply ashamed. My part in the engagement at Sheffield was strictly defensive, being merely part of a party that was out foraging for provisions when

*we were ambushed. I humbly ask the mercy and pardon of
the most gracious and loving fatherly Governor and
Council.*

"Peter will never sign that," I said. "It's all lies. He was
one of the best fighters we had."

"He's going to sign it if I have to take a club to him. He's
got to humble himself, he's got to grovel in front of the
Governor's Council. That's what they want to see him do."

"He won't sign it," I said. "He couldn't stand to grovel."

"It's easier to grovel than to hang," she said. She was
right. He signed it. "He didn't like it very much, but he did
it," she said when she got back. She got Uncle Billy Conkey to take the letter to Boston, because he was an important man around our part and hadn't been in any of the
actual fighting, although he'd helped provision us. Along
with it, Uncle Billy took a letter from Nathaniel Austin,
and another one from Sheriff Porter, which said that it
would be dangerous to hang the men because the whole
county might rise again. Hardest for me to believe, she had
a letter from Mattoon himself. I guess they really were
afraid of starting up the rebellion all over again if even
Mattoon would try to save Peter's neck. Maybe Mattoon
only wanted to be sure he got his forty shillings back—with
interest.

So we waited. The days passed and no word from Boston. All we could do was wait, and finally on the 19th of
June, two days before the execution, Uncle Billy came
back from Boston. It was no good: The men were to be
hanged on schedule.

That night Molly and I sat in the kitchen talking about it.

It was a nice night—warm and balmy, with the peepers going like mad outside. It sure was the wrong kind of night to talk about Peter dying. "What can we do?" I said. "It's pretty hopeless."

"No," she said. "It's never hopeless. "We're going to get him out of jail."

"I don't see how," I said. "They're not just locked up in jail, they're shackled to the wall. And a guard outside besides."

"The guard is only sixteen. He's not very smart, either. Maybe we can get around him."

"If you and Abby Austin got him into a conversation, maybe I could sneak around behind him and knock him out with a club."

"I'm not sure that would work," she said.

"Do you know the guard pretty well?" I asked.

"Sure. I've been going over there regularly for four months. His name is Abel Holman. It wouldn't be hard to get him into a conversation."

"Maybe we can come up with a better idea," I said.

"Maybe," she said.

The next morning, June 20th, the day before Peter was to be hanged, we took the little ones over to the tavern where Uncle Billy could look after them. Then we got up a package of food and a large jug of rum. Uncle Billy gave us a couple of good files. Molly pushed one of them into a loaf of bread. It left a mark where it went in, but you wouldn't notice it. I put the other one in my pocket. We'd have to see how things went. That afternoon we walked into Northampton.

Chapter Fourteen

THE THING THAT GOT ME WAS THE HUGE crowd that had come into Northampton to see Peter and Nathaniel Austin hanged. It was like a holiday. They were laughing and getting drunk. Sometimes, as we walked through the streets toward the jail, we heard people making jokes about it—how there was a lot of "suspense" in a hanging, because the prisoners were going to be "suspended" from a rope. It was pretty terrible to hear. I couldn't understand it. "I thought these people were all Regulators," I said. "I thought they were all on Peter's side."

Molly shook her head. She looked pretty mean. "People like a hanging. It makes them feel glad it isn't them."

We got to the jail. It was a wooden building made of squared logs. There were a few small windows in it, and bars in the windows. There was one door in front. An older man was on guard. He unlocked the door and let us in. We went into a small room with a couple of doors off it. The guard unlocked one of the doors, which opened on another small room. Peter and Nathaniel Austin were inside. Each of them had an iron ring around his ankle. A chain ran from the rings to beams in the wall, where they were fastened with great staples. Abby Austin was already there, talking to Nathaniel.

It was the first time I'd seen Peter since the fighting at Sheffield. It made me feel awful to see him chained up like an ox. He hadn't been able to shave since he'd been locked up. "What a beard you've got," I said.

"I understand they'll trim it tomorrow. It gets in the way of the noose."

It was a joke, but it made me feel sick.

"Who's that on guard duty?" Molly said. "Where's that boy?"

"He comes on later," Peter said. "He'll be on the night shift."

She kissed him. We all talked for a while. It was hard to think of things to say. Finally Molly said, "We'll be back later. Keep up your courage."

We left. Abby Austin came with us. There was nothing we could do until dark; we had to wait until Abel Holman came on duty, anyway. We wandered around town for a little while, but we couldn't stand the way everybody was making a holiday out of it, so we walked a mile or so out of town and sat under a tree at the edge of a field. "I still can't understand why people would act that way," I said. "I mean, roaring around and drinking when somebody on their side is going to be hanged."

"I think they're drinking so much because underneath they feel disgusted with themselves for coming out to see a man die."

"It's going to make it easier for the men to get away if everybody's drunk," Abby said.

We ate a little and then lay down to rest in the shade of

the tree. The sun was hot on the hay field, and raising the smell of the growing grass. I tried to just lie there and smell it, to keep my thoughts away from what was going to happen. We stayed there for a couple of hours, and then it began to get dark. We got up and walked back into town. There were throngs around the tavern singing and drinking, and lights were on everywhere. We slipped past the singing people to the jail.

Abel Holman was out front, leaning on the jail wall and picking his teeth with a twig. His musket rested against the wall beside him. "Hello, Molly," he said. "Hello, Abby."

Molly gave Abel a big smile. "Hello," she said. "Abel, this is my brother, Justin."

We shook hands. "You going to see Peter?"

"In a minute," I said. "I think I'd better have a drink of rum first." I unwrapped the food pack and took out the rum bottle. It was a full quart. I put the bottle to my lips, tipped back my head, and pretended to take a long drink. Then I handed the bottle to Molly and wiped off my lips. "You'd better have one, too, Molly." Molly pretended to drink and then she gave the bottle to Abby Austin and she tipped the bottle back, too. I took the bottle from her and started to wrap it up in the food parcel. Then I said, "Hey, Abel, how about you? Want a drink?"

He looked at me and then at the bottle. He wanted it, all right. "I'm not supposed to drink on duty."

"I wouldn't let that bother me," I said. "The whole town is drunk. Nobody will ever know."

He hesitated. "Well, no, I'd better not."

I shrugged. "It's no skin off my nose. I think I'll just have another." I pretended to drink again. When I was finished I sort of gestured toward Abel with the bottle. "Sure?" I said.

"Is anyone looking?"

"It's pitch dark, Abel. Nobody can see you."

He took the bottle, tipped it back hastily, and drank. The strong liquor made him cough. "Take a big one," I said. "There's plenty." He took another swallow.

"We're going in to see Peter," Molly said. Abel unlocked the door, and she and Abby went in. I stayed outside. Abel handed me back the bottle.

"Do you like this job?" I said.

"It's all right," he said.

"It must be pretty boring. I mean, just standing here all night long with nothing to do."

"It sure is."

I took another pretend drink and then I handed Abel the bottle. This time he took it without saying anything and had a long drink. That was three. I figured he'd begin to get woozy soon. We had lots of time. We had all night. So I stood there making conversation with him about his job, and what the General Court was doing, and so forth; and every once in a while I'd pretend to take a drink and he'd take a real one. After a bit Molly came out again and joined in the game. Faintly, from inside the jail, I could hear the soft sound of filing. The bottle kept going around; and before an hour was up Abel was leaning against the wall of the jail, shaking his head and blinking. "I don't feel so good," he said. The musket slid down the wall and fell onto the ground. He let it lie there. "I feel terrible," he said. He belched. And then suddenly he staggered around the corner of the jail. I could hear him throwing up. We waited, Molly and I, until he finished. There was silence. I tiptoed around the corner. Abel was lying face up on the ground, snoring. He'd be sleeping for a good long time.

Now we ran back to the jail. Peter had cut himself free of his shackles and was kneeling in front of Nathaniel Austin, filing at the chain. "I'll have this one off in ten minutes," he said. "It's only iron, it's not steel."

Molly nodded. "Justin, you stay outside and keep watch." Then she and Abby began to take off their dresses. I went outside and knelt down at the corner of the jail where I could keep an eye on Abel Holman and still see anybody coming up to the front. In my nose was the smell of rum and vomit. I didn't like that very much, but I wanted to stay close to Abel so I could whack him over the head if he started to wake up. I knelt there, waiting, listening to the distant shouting and singing of the drinkers and the soft sound of the file cutting iron, and then suddenly the jail door swung open and out ran two figures. One of them was wearing women's clothing. This one glanced back and gave me a little wave. It was Nathaniel Austin. He and Abby had changed clothing. In a moment they disappeared in the dark.

I leaped to my feet and ran back into the jail. Peter and Molly were standing there, both half-undressed. Peter was hastily putting his own clothes back on. "I can't get into Molly's dress. We shouldn't have wasted time trying."

Then there was a sort of croaking noise from the door. We all spun around. Abel Holman was standing there. His face was covered with sweat. "Holy God," he said. Then he turned and ran. I dashed after him and we burst out into the night with me just a few feet behind him. "Help," he shouted. "Jail break. Help." He was still drunk and wobbling as he ran. I closed in on him and dove onto his back. He pitched forward on his face. When we hit, I bounced off him. He raised up to his knees. "Help," he cried. I leaped on him again, flung him to the ground, slapped my hand over his mouth, and lay across his body to keep him still. There was a shout somewhere and the sound of running feet.

"If you make any noise, I'll strangle you," I said. He lay still. He wasn't in much condition to defend himself. The running feet were coming closer. "Peter," I shouted. "Somebody's coming." Five seconds later Peter came flying out of the jail as fast as he could go. Molly was right after him. They swung off into the darkness and as they did so two men came wheeling up the street.

"They got away," somebody shouted. "Stop them." They raced past where I was lying over the body of Abel Holman, but then there were more men coming and I jumped to my feet and began to run myself, heading through the dark streets away from town. All I could do was pray that Peter had got away. It didn't matter about Molly—they weren't going to hang her.

I zigzagged through one street and another until I was clear of town, and then I found a barn and slipped inside to sleep. It was a warm night, I was tired, but I dozed only in bits and pieces the rest of the night.

At first light I got up and out of the barn. It was hot already, and it was going to be muggy. I started walking back into Northampton to see what I could find out. I was hungry, but there was no way I could get anything to eat. As I came into town, I kept to the side streets. I figured

Abel Holman had told people what had happened to him and they'd be on the watch for me. But nobody in Northampton knew me, and I figured I'd be safe unless Abel himself spotted me. Still, I wasn't going to expose myself more than necessary.

Finally, I came to a tavern where two or three men were lounging around outside. I stopped. "Excuse me," I said politely. "Does anybody know what time the hangings are?"

"Hanging, you mean. There'll only be one. There was a jail break last night."

"Which one did they catch? Was it Nathaniel Austin or that McColloch fellow?"

"Austin," another man said.

"No, I heard it was McColloch."

"I swear they said it was Austin."

"Thanks, anyway," I said. So I still didn't know. I continued to walk on into town, heading more or less for the place where they'd put up the gallows. A couple of times more I stopped to listen to gossip or ask questions, but it was always the same—there were a lot of rumors around, but nobody knew for sure what had happened or who had got away. I spent the morning keeping out of the way and trying to scrape up something to eat, but I didn't have any luck at that.

Then, exactly at noon, there came the sound of drums and a great movement in the streets toward the Northampton church. I slipped into the crowd and followed along. The mob at the church was enormous. There seemed to be thousands of people gathered there. There wasn't any way they could all fit inside the church. They

were standing around outside, jostling for a better view.
They had built a platform near the side window of the
church. The sound of the drums was coming closer. People
began craning their heads over the crowd, and in a moment
we could see a double line of marching militiamen, with
drummers in the front, coming toward us. I waited, my
heart pounding. The procession came closer. In a moment
I could see, behind the drummers, two ministers walking
solemnly along. Behind them I caught a glimpse of another
figure. I strained to see who it was, and when it came closer
I saw that it was Peter. They had caught him.

The militiamen were now heading straight into the
crowd, which gave way to let them pass as water gives way
before a boat. First came the drummers, playing a dreary,
thumping march; then the double files began, then the
ministers, and then Peter. They had cut off his beard, but
they had not shaved him, and his face was hairy. He was
pale, but he was standing straight to show that he was not
afraid. He passed. He didn't see me, or if he did he made
no sign. And I had been watching him so closely that I
didn't notice until he had gone by, that Molly was coming
along behind him. There was a smudge of dirt on her face
and her hands were tied behind her back. I couldn't believe
it. They were going to make her watch her husband get
hanged.

They pushed Peter up onto the platform at the side of
the church, and then the ministers went inside and stood
up in an open balcony window where they could be seen
and heard by the enormous crowd. One of them began a
sermon. I couldn't hear him very well and anyway, I wasn't
in any mind to concentrate on it. All I could think was that

in a little while Peter would be dead. It seemed impossible to believe.

I couldn't see Molly. They hadn't put her up on the platform, but had kept her down in the lines of the militiamen. The sermon went on and on. The two ministers spoke in turns. I don't know how long it lasted, it was nearly endless it seemed, hours long, anyway. But finally the ministers came to an end. Some militiamen made Peter jump down from the platform and prodded him back into the double column again. The drums began to beat, and off they marched for the gallows. The crowd surged along with the procession, ahead, behind, and alongside the double file of militiamen. The people were shouting and talking and drinking rum from flasks. The whole thing was very exciting to them, and they chattered and joked with each other as they went along.

The militiamen reached the gallows. It was set in an open square, just a platform about six feet off the ground with a wooden arm reaching up ten feet and a heavy rope dangling from the arm. There was a coffin on the platform, with the sheriff standing beside it. As warm and humid as it was, I was as cold inside as I had been all winter, and I could hardly get my breath except in little gasps. Four of the militiamen climbed up on the platform and sort of pulled Peter up there. I couldn't see Molly through the crowd. I wondered if she would keep her eyes closed.

The drums went on beating. The militiamen on the platform were holding Peter tight. The sheriff's deputy slipped the heavy noose over his head and fixed it around his neck. He was rough in doing it, and I could almost feel the rope myself scraping down over my forehead.

Suddenly the drums stopped. The crowd went silent. Peter stood there staring straight ahead. The militiamen stepped back to the corners of the platform, out of the way but in readiness in case Peter tried to make a break for it. There was no sound from the crowd. They were frozen. In the distance a dog barked. Cold sweat was running down my face and into my eyes, and I had to blink to see. Then the sheriff stepped forward. He reached into his coat and pulled out a paper. He began to read:

> *By the order of the Governor and the Council of the Commonwealth of Massachusetts, in their infinite mercy, the man Peter McColloch is to be reprieved . . .*

I began to cry, shaking and sobbing with my hands over my face, the tears leaking out between my fingers.

Chapter Fifteen

OF COURSE, IT WASN'T QUITE OVER, NOT then. There were more legalities to be got through until finally a full pardon came and Peter was free to go home. But when Molly and I went back up to Pelham that night, we knew he was safe. It was clear that the government was scared to hang any of the Regulators for fear of stirring up trouble again. They'd come as close as they'd dared, just to throw a scare into everybody. But in the end they hadn't dared to go all the way.

After that, things began to improve. We had a lot of our own men in the General Court now, and bit by bit they passed laws that improved our situation. The steady stream of taxes slowed down, and the heavy expenses for court costs and lawyers were reduced. A man had a chance of keeping his farm if he worked hard.

And so it was over. In time, people came to call it Shays' Rebellion, and to write it up in books. In later years, I was proud that I'd been a part of it, and if anybody asked me about it, I'd tell the whole story from beginning to end. Of course, by then I wasn't living on Peter's farm anymore. I'd been able to buy a farm of my own.

So that was that. I married and had children of my own and worked hard, and after a while I was able to buy a second farm, and I prospered. But every once in a while, I thought about Shays' Rebellion, and what we'd done, and I would wonder what anybody had learned from it.

One thing I had learned was that there wasn't much point in going out to be a hero, because you never know how something is going to look to everybody else. You might as well go along and do your best, and not worry about who's the hero and who isn't.

A second thing that came out of it had to do with the making of the United States itself. At the time of Shays' Rebellion, most of the people figured that it was important for the states to keep power to themselves and not turn it over to the Federal Government. They felt that the states should be more important than the Federal Government and have the major say in most everything, like taxes, and the militia. But Shays' Rebellion scared a lot of people. They decided that if we didn't have a strong Federal Government there might be other revolts coming along, keeping things in a turmoil all the time. And that's the way it finally came out. So, as you can see, what we did in the winter of 1786 and 1787 had a big effect on the future of the nation.

And one last thing that we learned out of it was that if you don't take the trouble to vote your own representatives to the government, the government is likely to do a lot of things you don't like. If we'd sent our people to the General Court in the first place, we might have never had to fight.

But then again, we might have. If there hadn't been a rebellion, maybe nobody much in western Massachusetts would have got fired up enough to go out and vote. This was a question I never could decide. Would we ever have got our grievances redressed if we hadn't shown the government that we were willing to fight?

How much of this book is true?

Historians are often very clever at reconstructing the past so we can understand it, but even the cleverest of them will admit that there are many things we cannot be sure about. This is true of Shays' Rebellion—we cannot be certain of every detail. Nonetheless, as far as we have been able to understand, all the major, and many of the minor, events that are portrayed in this book happened just as we have described them. The battle at the Springfield Arsenal, the rout of Shays' forces at Petersham, the fighting at Sheffield, and even the suffocation of Levi Bullock and Tom Mayo in the potato hole are taken directly from eye-witness accounts. Uncle Billy Conkey was real, and his tavern still existed in the town of Pelham into the early part of this century. There are still Conkeys in that area today. Major Mattoon was also the sort of River God we have described him as. However, we do not know that he was quite as unsympathetic a person as we have made him out to be. Nathaniel Austin is also real, and did the things we have him do in the escape from the jail. So were the petitions that were sent to Boston and the efforts the women made to get their husbands pardoned.

However, Justin Conkey is a made-up character. There were plenty of boys around who lived the way he did, and some of them fought in Shays' Rebellion, but Justin's role in the events of the rebellion are fictitious. Molly, too, is made up. But Peter McColloch has some basis in fact. We created him by combining two men who did exist, Peter Wilcox and Henry McColloch. McColloch was jailed for his part in the rebellion, did attempt an escape with the help of his wife, who got the sixteen-year-old guard Abel Holman drunk. (Poor Abel was put in jail for letting the men escape.) He also went through the ordeal of the false execution just as we have described it. We cannot say, however, that either of the men who make up Peter were like him; we simply do not know.

The matter of the language in which this story is told is another question. Historians do not know exactly how people of Justin's time talked. Therefore, we have told the story in more or less modern English to make it comprehensible to our readers.

About the Authors

James Lincoln Collier has written many
books for children, including *Give Dad My
Best* and *Planet Out of the Past*. Mr. Collier
has also contributed more than five hundred
articles to such publications as *The New York
Times Magazine*, *Reader's Digest*, and *Boys'
Life*. Along with his brother, Christopher Collier, he has written six books, the most recent
of which is *War Comes to Willie Freeman*.
James Lincoln Collier lives in New York City.

Christopher Collier is Professor of History
at the University of Connecticut. His field
is early American history, especially the
history of Connecticut and the American
Revolution. He and his wife live in Orange,
Connecticut.